EMILY ANTOINETTE

MANEATER

A MONSTERS OF MOONVALE NOVELLA

To anyone who wants a succubus girlfriend to take control and tell them how good they are or anyone who wants a sweet cinnamon roll guy to worship them. Or both!

CONTENT NOTES

Hello there! I hope you're ready for an 80's monster romance with lots of fluffy romance and hot spice. Maneater is a prequel to my upcoming book, Behold Her, but both can be read as standalone stories.

Maneater features open-door, consensual spicy encounters, including: stripping, lap dancing, feeding off of arousal, a bisexual virgin MMC, a pansexual FMC, D/s dynamics (soft domme succubus/submissive witch), edging, praise, sex magic gone wrong, tail play, anal sex, face-sitting, breeding (without pregnancy), and tentacles.

Much of the story is cozy and sweet, however it includes discussions of: past relationship trauma, sexual coercion, slut shaming, fears about coming out, social anxiety, and worries about sexual performance.

If you have any questions, please feel free to reach out to me at emilyantoinetteauthor@gmail.com!

1

SHANE

You *can do this. Just go inside, say hello, and ask if they'll put your flyer up for you. Easy peasy. The worst thing that will happen is they say no. Like the last three places you tried...*

Maybe I should just give up and call it a day.

"Hey man, you in or you out?"

I startle, tearing my eyes away from the collection of flyers for bands, psychics, and dog walkers posted in the shop window to turn toward the brusque voice. A short pallid guy wearing a leather jacket far too heavy for this unseasonably warm autumn day glares at me, gesturing to the shop door he's holding open.

"Oh right, sorry!" I swallow down my defeatist thinking. I need more work. That won't happen if I hide at home and don't keep trying to market myself. "In!"

I hustle to the open door, squeezing past him and attempting to not snag my sweater vest on the metal spikes jutting from his jacket. He lets out a huffed exhale once I've grabbed the door and heads off down the sidewalk. "Thanks," I call after him weakly, but he doesn't acknowledge it. Hopefully, the people inside the store are friendlier.

I head inside and the bell hanging above the door rings out as it shuts behind me, scraping against my already frayed nerves. With a deep breath in to stabilize myself, I push up my glasses and scan the shop.

Rows of bookshelves fill most of the claustrophobic space, the aisles barely wide enough for someone to pass through. Display cases holding an eclectic mix of crystals, figurines, and candles line the perimeter. I take a step away from the door and try to ignore the powerful scent of incense tickling my nose, resisting the urge to fade into the shadows between the bookcases.

You'd think a witch like me would feel at home here. But this den of new age pursuits is far from my comfort zone. I'm someone you'd expect to see digging through a card catalog or stuck in a computer lab, not lighting incense and gazing into crystal balls.

Wandering past books about discovering your chakras and manuals on tarot, I head toward the back of the shop, where I can sense the only other occupants are located. There's a small counter with a cash register in front of a beaded curtain leading into a back room, but no one is behind it. There's no bell to ring, so I idly scan a display case of oddities nearby while I wait for someone to return. A miniature pewter figurine of a wizard holding a crystal ball catches my eye—it could be a fun prop for my biweekly D&D

game. I wince as I check the price. Way too expensive for what amounts to a silly trinket. If I can get some more work, then maybe I'll stop back in and pick it up.

A couple of minutes pass with no sign of someone working here. I debate leaving, but push that anxiety-fueled thought aside. I inhale deeply and channel some of my magic to heighten my senses further, and after a moment, I can make out a small gasp from the back room and the sound of flesh slapping.

Oh. *Oh my.*

My face heats and I duck back between the bookcases. No wonder no one greeted me when I entered. I should come back later. Flustered, I knock into a display of "magic infused" candles as I turn to move away. They clatter to the ground and someone curses in the back room.

"Be right there!" a high-pitched voice calls, followed by rustling and murmured curses. As I try to fix the toppled candles, a ruddy man in a rumpled business suit strides past me toward the exit with a curt nod. I blink back up and notice he's forgotten to do his zipper. "Sir, your fly..." I call out, but he's already out the door.

"Welcome to Magick Soul! How can I help you, young man? Oh my! It looks like you had a bit of a run in with our fortune candles."

I turn to see a middle-aged woman smiling down at me, her light brown cheeks darkened and a sheen of sweat on her brow. A long black dress hangs loosely on her slender frame, and a large metal ankh necklace dangles as she bends over to help me with the remaining candles I've disturbed.

"Maybe it was the universe telling me I could use some." I return her smile with a sheepish one of my own and stand, brushing the front of my slacks to smooth them out.

"We all could use some more fortune, whether it be money or

luck. But I sense that you're here for something else." She gives me a knowing look, and I can't tell if she's using a well-honed mystical shopkeeper persona or if she actually has the gift of seeing.

"Oh? What would that be?" I test her, starting the dance that paranormals do to determine if they're among their kind. Most of us use charms to disguise our nature, which makes it harder to discern. But better that than accidentally reveal ourselves to an unsuspecting human and risk the safety that hiding from humans has afforded monsters. If she's a witch like me, then putting up a business flyer here might end up working out even more than I'd hoped.

She laughs and holds my gaze instead of scanning over me to get a better read like a fake intuitive would. "You're new in the city and looking for work. To advertise your services. You're also looking for a group of like-minded practitioners, though I don't think you came here expecting to find that."

All of that could be generic nonsense, but the intensity of her gaze says otherwise. "Impressive! Though, I suppose the flyers I'm holding could have tipped you off about me hoping to advertise here." I hold up the stack of papers in my hand and wiggle them a bit, keeping the text facing toward me.

"True. As a private detective, you no doubt could find many reasons it was observation and not intuition." She winks at me and I barely hold back from showing surprise at her guess at my profession.

"Well, I figured you'd want an example of my skill set before letting me put up a flyer," I say with a shrug, holding one out to her.

She takes it with another knowing smile and reads over it. "Nice to meet you, Shane. I'm Liz. And I'll be happy to hang this up in the shop under one condition."

I rub the back of my neck, flushing at my rudeness for not asking her name or offering an introduction of my own. "A pleasure to meet you, Liz. What would that condition be?"

"It's the other reason you're here." She turns and walks back to the counter, without offering more of an explanation.

I follow her, watching as she digs through a drawer under the counter. "Uh...what reason is that?"

"You're looking for a group." Liz scans the shop and lowers her voice. "A coven."

I raise a brow. "I'm not a wiccan."

She huffs and gives me a dismissive wave. "Of course not. That's not what I'm talking about."

When I keep my expression blank, she huffs again. "Yes, yes, you did good with secretive double-speak, but we can dispense with that. You infused your flyers with a magic signal for paranormals. You're a witch. I'm a witch. So when I say you're looking for a coven, I mean one of true magic practitioners."

"Oh." Damn, I wasn't expecting that. A nervous laugh bubbles out of me. "I forgot about the flyers..."

Liz pats my hand. "That's okay, cutie. I know you were a bit flustered after what you walked in on. Which I apologize for. I don't normally take my pleasure during work hours, but Jeffrey's been slammed with meetings and it's the only time outside of coven meetings we have time to—"

I hold up a hand to stop her. "No need to explain! Wait, he's also part of the coven?"

"Yes. Did you think that only new-age ladies like me practiced? Because your appearance doesn't exactly scream 'magic' either."

I glance down at my orange and gray sweater vest and dark pants, my glasses slipping down the bridge of my nose and a lock of my rumpled red hair falling into my eyes. "No, I suppose a nerd like me doesn't give off those vibes."

"Right. Clothes don't matter. Underneath, we're all the same. Just bodies channeling the divine energy of the universe into magic." She gives me a quick once over, her eyes lingering on my hips for a moment. "Though some bodies are a bit more divine than others, aren't they, Shane?" she adds with a wink.

Gods, now I'm really turning red. I cough and mumble something in agreement, unable to meet her gaze.

"We're meeting here tomorrow night at 9. There's a door around the side of the building that leads to the lower level, and I'll make sure you can enter. There's a special celebration happening, actually! It'll be the perfect time for you to meet everyone."

I'm torn. While I've been meaning to find a coven, the offer throws me off. Shouldn't they have some kind of application or vetting process for new members? But with my hermit-like tendencies, when am I going to meet another witch as friendly and open as Liz? Before I can let my trepidation talk me out of agreeing, I nod. "Sure, thanks."

"Wonderful! Now, pass me that stack of flyers. I'll put one up in here and pass some on to other monster friends that own businesses in town. Before you know it, you'll have more jobs than you know what to do with."

"Wow, thank you so much, Liz!" My smile and thanks are much more earnest this time. I've been struggling to get my business off the ground and today is the first time I've gotten any real traction since moving to the city. Maybe those fortune candles rubbed off on me.

"Sure thing, cutie. See you tomorrow night at 9! Don't worry about bringing anything other than yourself." She eyes me appreciatively again. Her flirting is a little off-putting, but I shake that feeling away and wave goodbye. I don't get it, but I'm not about to complain about someone finding me attractive. Sure, I'm decent looking, but I'm no buff paragon of manliness. Just an average skinny ginger who rarely remembers to go to the gym.

She's probably just being nice to the awkward witch who wandered into her shop like a lost puppy.

2

SHANE

*O*r maybe Liz really is *interested in me.*

I've just made it down the steep stairs leading to the lower level of Magick Soul when the older woman tugs me into a hug, pressing herself against my chest and lingering for a moment too long as she inhales. "Mmm, so glad you decided to come, Shane!"

My face flames as she lets me go, eyes darting toward the stairs. I'd gone back and forth all day about whether I should come to the coven meeting. I've been fine practicing magic on my own since I moved to the city about three months ago. But my curiosity got the best of me. Now, as Liz grabs my hand and leads me down a cold concrete hall, I'm wondering if I made the wrong decision.

This whole place is a lot more murder dungeon-y than I'd expected after seeing the shop upstairs.

That feeling only intensifies when we enter a barren concrete chamber, where about a dozen other people mill around chatting. I don't have time to take in any more details before the red-cheeked business man from yesterday steps up to us and extends a hand to me.

"You must be Shane. Welcome. I'm Jeffrey." His white button-down shirt is rolled up at the sleeves and an expensive-looking gold watch gleams in the low light as I shake his hand. He must've come here right from work.

"Uh, hi! Nice to meet you."

"Good work with this one, Liz." Jeffrey nudges me playfully and grins at us.

My sense of unease deepens. "How do you mean?" I scan the room, looking for the best path out, but people are standing directly in front of the only exit.

"Oh, Jeffrey's just another appreciator of nice bodies," Liz says with a shrug.

I tug at the collar of my shirt, which suddenly feels too tight. More people have flirted with me in the past two days than in my entire life, and it's setting off alarm bells in my head. I shouldn't have come here tonight. "Oh. Right. Uh, is there a restroom I could—"

"Liz! Jeff! And this fine specimen must be Shane!" A muscular man with tan brown skin interrupts my feeble escape attempt, clapping a hand on my back hard enough to knock the breath out of me. "I'm Derek. I'm leading tonight's ceremony. You've picked the perfect time to join us. We've been planning this for months, but needed one more body for the ritual. And then you walk into Liz's shop, like a gift from the Gods themselves." Derek flashes his bright white teeth in a smile that I'm sure he means to be charming, but only enhances the creepiness of what he just said.

Great job, Shane. Of course the friendly woman wasn't eyeing your bod because she thought you were hot. She just needed a body for whatever weird ritual they're doing. Please don't let it be a ritual sacrifice. I still have so much living to do. I don't want to die a virgin. Oh gods, do they know I'm a virgin and need my blood?

"Earth to Shane? You okay there, cutie?" Liz's voice cuts through my spiraling thoughts. When I register her face in front of mine, her expression twisted in concern, I nod and gulp in a breath.

"Y-yeah. Just, uh, a little nervous. What exactly is this ritual?"

"Oh sweetie, don't be nervous! No one here will bite—unless you ask them to." She laughs at her own joke, but I barely manage a weak smile. "Don't worry about the ritual either, just stand on your spot on the circle and repeat the words when Derek tells you to. I think you're really going to enjoy it. In fact, I *know* you're going to find something you crave tonight."

Something I crave? I blink back at her, unable to formulate a coherent response.

"Looks like we're getting started! Go on, get your cute butt over on the spot next to Jeffrey." Liz smacks my ass and I stumble away, flushing.

Seeing no means of getting out of this room that doesn't involve pushing through at least three people, I reluctantly stand on a runed dot on the perimeter of the large circle drawn in white chalk on the concrete floor. Concentric rings and lines weave through the design, all painstakingly measured and precise. I don't recognize the pattern, but I do most of my magic through enchantment rather than rituals that would require a magic circle.

"Get ready for the night of your life, Shane," Jeffrey says with a wink as he loosens his shirt collar, then turns to focus on Derek on the other side of the circle. The muscular man holds a red, leather-bound tome and looks out over the gathered group with a feral grin.

"Thank you all for coming tonight. This is something our humble little coven has worked tirelessly to bring to life. And with Margaret's last-minute illness, we thought we'd have to cancel and try again in a few months. But thanks to our newest member, Shane, we don't have to wait!" He pauses and gestures toward me.

I almost flinch as twelve pairs of eyes all land on me and wave feebly under the weight of their eager stares. Guess there's no backing out now. Unless I fake a sudden onset of food poisoning...

"Hah! Shane's shy, but I'm sure he'll warm up after the ritual, right?" Everyone laughs, but I don't get the joke. "Anyway, enough of me babbling. Let's get this going!"

A few people let out soft cheers of excitement and Derek waits for the room to grow quiet before he cracks open the tome and begins to chant. His voice starts so softly that I have to strain, even with my magic-enhanced hearing, to make out anything. It grows louder and louder as he reads until his booming voice echoes through the stone room. The language sounds demonic, but it's an ancient dialect I never had a reason to study. I can only translate a handful of words.

Come...Give...Release...

Fuck, this doesn't sound good. The chalk lines on the floor glow like embers, and Derek nods. "Speak with me. Call it forth."

Call *what* forth? Panic lances through me and I instinctively go take a step back, but an invisible barrier locks me where I stand. Shit, whatever they're summoning needs containment. My mind races as I try to recall any counterspells that will help me get past the barrier before I'm trapped for good.

"Come to us," Derek calls out, and the group repeats. I don't, because screw whatever they're doing, I don't want any part of it. Gods, if I make it out of here alive, I'm never trying to make new friends again. I'm just going to stay in my apartment and watch MTV.

"We bind you, dark one." Again the group echoes Derek. The circle glows brighter, the center ring erupting into magical flame. "Join us. Unleash the desires within."

Terror surges through me at whatever's about to come through. Most likely a demon, given the incantation and powerful bindings. While some demons have integrated with paranormal society, others—especially the more dangerous ones—stick to their own realm. There's no way of knowing which kind these fools are summoning. With my luck, it'll be the "murder first, ask questions later" type.

To hell with this. I'm not dying tonight! I gather up all my magic, using brute force to push against the barrier holding me in this damn circle. It bends and with a pained grunt I shove even harder, finally breaking through and stumbling away from the circle, searing white-hot pain surging across my skin as I do. I fall on my ass and scramble backwards just as the entire magic circle glows with purple, sparkling energy and an otherworldly sound rips through the room.

Everyone gasps as the creature they've summoned appears in the center of the circle. Large pink bat-like wings unfurl to reveal the most gorgeous being I've ever laid eyes on. Flawless pink skin, curling horns jutting out from a wild mane of black hair, angry violet eyes, and plush red lips twisted in a furious scowl. The demon is completely nude, save for a tiny g-string that glitters in the low light and a pair of platform heels. My cock hardens as I take in her ample breasts and thick, powerful hips and thighs. Her long, spade-tipped tail lashes in agitation, drawing my gaze to her perfectly rounded ass.

She looks furious and ready to kill. Fuck, I need to get out of here while I can. But I'm transfixed. They've summoned a dark goddess and I'll willingly be sacrificed if it means I can stay in her presence.

3

Y*ou have got to be fucking kidding me.*
I spin around to get my bearings, eliciting gasps from the idiots circled around me. Twelve idiots, to be precise, all staring at me with rapturous wonder. We're in some dank, low-lit basement.

Great. You'd think they'd at least haul some mattresses or cushions down to the space they're summoning a lust demon.

The witch holding a tome, who must be their leader, kneels on his spot on the exterior ring of the magic circle and the rest follows suit. As they do, I notice one space on the circle is empty and there's the remnant of a tear in the binding magic. Someone got cold feet. Or needed to piss before their planned fuck fest began.

Even with the weakened spot, the barrier is too solid for me to escape.

"Oh dark mistress, bless us with your gifts. We offer our bodies to you this night. Take what you will, and once you've sated yourself on our eager lusts, we will release the bindings." The leader strips off his t-shirt to reveal a finely chiseled torso and the others undress as well. The waves of lust pouring off of this group are almost enough to make me lightheaded with hunger, but I maintain my cold scowl as I glare at the one who spoke.

These damn sex magic cults always phrase things in a way that makes it sound like they're doing me a favor by hauling me to them with no warning, forcing me into my monster form, and then keeping me stuck there until I deign to fuck them. When I was younger, I got wrapped up in the drama of it. But now? These assholes are going to get me fired if I don't get out of here and back to the club soon. I glance down at my g-string and my simmering anger boils over when I see the crisp twenty-dollar bill a patron was about to stick there is gone.

"Silence!" I shout, my voice cutting through the babbling of their leader and echoing off the empty walls. A few of them gasp as I spread my wings out and get into an intimidating stance, despite my tits being out. Imagining that they're each just tiny bugs about to be crushed under my heel, I growl. Some start to shake and I make a mental note to thank my cousin Xae for teaching me that visualization. Scaring people doesn't come naturally to me, but sometimes it's necessary. "You've brought me here against my will. And you think to ask me for my favor?"

A middle-aged woman blinks up at me rapidly, her small breasts already bared and heaving with anticipation. "Please. We need you. Use us." Her words come out as a moan and she seems on the verge of coming just from me being in the room with her. I lick my lips involuntarily, tasting her desire, and she lets out a needy whimper. "*Please.*"

"You don't deserve me. If you want to fuck, fuck each other. I have places to be." I roll my eyes and cross my arms over my chest, blocking my breasts from these pervs' view. If they want to ogle me, they can come see me strip like any decent person would. Not trap me in their sex cult lair.

"No! You can't leave, we've worked so hard!" their leader gasps, shaking his head. He stands, his unimpressive cock hard against his stomach. "We won't release you until you give us what we need." The others surrounding me nod and murmur their assent.

Looks like intimidation won't work. I really don't want to expend the energy needed to charm them into releasing me. I'll be too exhausted to go back to work if I have to charm all of them. Maybe I should just fuck them. At least then I'd get out of here, not completely drained. I'm about to tell the woman on the verge of an orgasm to crawl to me and lick my pussy when a new voice cuts through the room from a dark corner outside the circle.

"What the fuck is wrong with you people? You're seriously telling a succubus she has to fuck you for her freedom? Gods, do you even hear yourselves?" I focus in on the darkness and raise a brow in surprise when a lanky redhead emerges. He must be the one that broke out of the circle before I arrived.

My first thought when I see him is that he's adorable, his cheeks flushed with indignation under his large glasses. His voice wavers a bit as he speaks, but it's got a nice low rasp to it that doesn't fit his appearance.

"You don't know what you're talking about, we—"

My champion practically growls in anger as he moves toward the circle, cutting off the shaking, desperate woman who was speaking. "Shut. Up."

A small shiver of desire runs down my spine at his command, surprising me.

He turns to me and frowns. Embarrassment and nerves radiate off of him, dampening the arousal he must feel in my presence. "Apologies, ma'am. If it's okay with you, I'll help you out of there."

I huff out a small laugh at him calling me ma'am, and give him a long once over. Up close, he's not as weak-looking as he appeared from a distance, but he'd still be so easy to command. I could bend him over and tease his—*wow*, rather thick cock judging by the bulge in his pants—until he begs me to fuck him. He flushes even more at my perusal, and I nod. He probably hopes that I'll suck him off out of gratitude, but at least he's offering to help.

He mutters an incantation and extends a hand through the circle, wincing as the invisible barrier sears his skin. It's impressive that he's able to push through despite the pain. *I wonder what other kinds of pain he could endure.*

Pushing that thought aside, I take his hand, and he gasps as my skin touches his. Lust spikes within him, so potent I'm on the edge of coming from it. For a moment I worry I misread his intentions, but he lets go right away once he's tugged me through the unpleasant heat of the barrier. The people in the circle behind me yell curses at him, but he ignores them and motions for me to follow him, then flips them off.

"Never hanging out with other witches again," he grumbles under his breath as he stomps up a steep set of stairs and through a heavy door out into the cool night air. He turns around and his eyes widen, like he forgot I was behind him. His throat works as he does his best to maintain eye contact with me and not drop his gaze to my bare tits. I wouldn't blame him if he did. After all, I'm designed to turn people on. And I like it—when it's on my own terms.

I smirk at him and step closer, licking my lips. He takes a stumbling step back, eyes falling for a second to watch my breasts sway before looking away.

"I'm so sorry, ma'am. What happened down there was inexcusable. You probably won't believe me when I tell you this, but it was my first meeting with them and I didn't know it was, uh, it was..."

I close the space between us and grab his chin, forcing him to look at me. He shudders with pleasure at my touch, but I can sense that warring with other emotions within him. Guilt and nerves, and something I can't quite place. "A sex magic cult?" I offer.

"Y-yes." He blinks rapidly at me, his glasses slipping down his nose. I release him, and he sways on his feet. A moment later, he reaches down and starts unbuttoning his shirt.

I roll my eyes. Guess he expects a reward for helping me, despite the innocent doe-eyed act. "You say you're not a part of their group, but here you are undressing as soon as I touch you. *Fine*. Get your dick out."

He makes a sputtering, choked sound and backs away again, tearing off his shirt and shoving it out toward me as his face flames. "N-no! I wanted to give you something to cover up with so you didn't have to stand out here n-naked."

I blink back at him in shock. He's seriously not asking a half-naked succubus for anything in return for his help?

When I don't take the shirt, he winces. "Shit. Right. Of course you can't wear this—your wings...I'm so sorry. You could, uh, wear it backwards? No, that's dumb, Shane..." His voice gets softer as he speaks until he's muttering to himself.

A smile twists my lips at his awkwardness. I grab his wrist, then take the shirt with my other hand, running a nail along the spellmark tattooed on my wrist that will let me turn back to my "human" form.

He turns away like he wants to preserve my modesty as I shift and shrug the shirt on. I can't button it all the way, and my tits threaten to pop the buttons, but I'm wearing this to make him more comfortable, not out of any sense of modesty. The scent of ozone from his magic and something like wood-smoke fills my nose. My nipples harden at the interesting, unique blend surrounding me. "Thanks...Shane, was it? You can turn around now."

"Uh, yeah. I'm Shane. Nice to meet you. Well, probably not nice for you given the circumstances, but uh..." He reaches his hand out and then thinks better of it, drawing it back to rub the back of his neck and clear his throat.

"A pleasure, Shane." I fill my voice with a husky purr just to taste the delightful shy arousal that surges from him as I do. "As much as I enjoy you calling me ma'am, my name is Xrixielle. Though my friends call me Elle."

"Xrixielle. That's a lovely name." He clears his throat again. "Do you need a ride somewhere? This part of the city isn't the safest late at night. Not that I think you can't handle yourself!"

A warm chuckle bubbles up in my throat. "A ride sounds great." I resist the urge to wink at him as I say it, but he still swallows heavily at the innuendo. "Do you know where Heaven's Door is?" I doubt he does, but all kinds of people go to strip clubs, so it's not out of the realm of possibility.

"No, but I've heard of it. Can you give me directions?"

"Mmm, I'd love to, Shane." The words come out of me in a low purr before I can stop them. Gods, I need to get off. Being around all of that lust is messing with my head and making me starving for more.

"Uh, I...um, great." Shane scrambles over to a station wagon and tugs open the passenger door for me. *Such a gentleman.*

I slide inside and surreptitiously undo two of the buttons so that my nipples peek out of the shirt while he's going around to get into the driver's seat. When he joins me in the car, Shane's eyes fall to my breasts and his throat works as a bloom of desire washes over him. I lean in a bit and lock eyes with him. "Thank you for your help tonight, Shane," I whisper, trailing my fingers across his bicep and up to tease at the sleeve of his undershirt.

"It's n-nothing." He leans in slightly and I sigh with anticipation, eager for release. A quick, wild fuck in his car sounds perfect. My clit pulses as the sizzling tension lingers between us, ready for him to break and give us both what we need.

But then he leans back and shakes his head, like he's trying to clear his lustful thoughts away.

"What they did was wrong. Disgusting. I'm sorry."

I sit back with a sigh, confused why his tongue isn't currently shoved down my throat. "It's okay. It happens."

His frown deepens. "No, it's not! Just because you're a succubus doesn't mean you're down to fuck anything that moves. I mean, you could if you wanted to. But it should be your choice!"

Now it's my turn to be flustered. "Well, yes...um, you're right. Thank you, Shane. You're a genuinely good guy, aren't you?"

He smiles shyly and runs a hand through his hair. "Just doing what anyone in their right mind would do."

Other than me providing directions, the drive to the club is awkward and silent. Neither of us seems to know what to say, and if he doesn't want to acknowledge the desire smothering us in this cramped car, I won't push him.

Though when he pulls up in front of Heaven's Door and cuts the engine, I can't resist leaning in to kiss him on the cheek. He inhales sharply as my lips scrape against the faint stubble on his jaw as I pull away, and it takes all my willpower not to crawl into his lap and grind against him like a teenager.

"You need me to walk you in?"

"You're too sweet. I'm fine. Though I'm afraid I'll need to hang on to your shirt."

"Oh, it's fine. You can keep it."

I give him a fake pout. "And here I was, hoping I could use your shirt to entice you to come see me sometime."

"Y-you, uh, you'd want me to come see you here?" He can barely get out the words.

I'd meant something outside of work, but the thought of this shy sweetheart watching me onstage is too delicious to resist. "Yes. I'm working again tomorrow night. Unless they fire me. But I'm sure I can use my charms to persuade them to keep me around. I want you to come see me. Will you come for me, Shane?"

His brow shoots up to his hairline and I swear I see his cock twitch in his pants. "Oh gods, uh, yes, I'll come for you—come see you. Tomorrow. If you're certain. I don't want to make you uncomfortable, Xrixielle."

"Not at all. But please, call me Elle. I can tell we're going to be much more than friends."

4

ELLE

"And then I asked him to *come for me*." I groan and cover my face with my free hand.

"You didn't!" Xae's cackling laugh almost blows out the speaker of my phone as I pace back and forth in my kitchen. "Oh gods, Elle," they wheeze out between more laughter.

"You're supposed to sympathize or to tell me what to do, not laugh at me, dickwad! I should've called one of our cooler cousins."

"Shut up. You know I'm the only cool one. But you're right...it's just...*Elle*. That poor boy probably came in his jeans the second you left."

I snort out a laugh, but my blood heats at the thought. I'm much more clear-headed now that I've slept off the inundation of desire from the stupid sex cultists, but there's a lingering ache between my thighs that didn't go away despite multiple sessions with my favorite vibrator. An ache that's directed toward the poor guy who was just trying to help.

"I bet he waited until he got home, at least. He seemed too polite to come in public."

"Do you think he'll show up? Do you want him to show up?"

I twist the spiral phone cord around my finger as I consider. "I... I wouldn't mind if he came."

"Hah, I bet you wouldn't."

"You know what I mean!" I giggle, a sound I haven't made in years. "But yeah, that too."

"Who would've known that your succubus bait was the shy, nerdy type?"

"Succubus bait?"

"Yeah, the type of person who's like catnip to you. That makes your pussy purr the most."

I groan at their terrible joke. "He's not..." I don't finish, because dammit, they're right. I haven't craved someone like this in years. Maybe ever. My job at Heaven's Door feeds me enough to feel satisfied and stable. But even after finishing my shift last night, I was still hungry. I feel like I'm going to burst out of my skin with the need to sate my lust for that unassuming witch.

"I doubt he'll show. He seemed too nice to actually be interested in a succubus once the haze of lust wore off."

"Fuck that shit. Sure, he probably was hypnotized by your bodacious bod at first, but anyone who spends more than a few minutes with you realizes you've got a personality to match. You deserve someone nice, Elle. Especially after your last few flings... after Gjler—the unspeakable ex."

Just hearing part of my fuckwad ex's name makes my stomach

churn, but I push it down. Fuck that asshole. I'm not going to let him ruin my self-esteem. "Yeah. I do. I deserve good things. Maybe Shane will show up!"

"He will! How could he possibly stay away?"

HE'S NOT COMING. It's past 11:30, and though I didn't specify a time, he should have shown by now. Every time I take the stage and don't see him out there, my heart sinks a little more. A bitter part of my mind resents Xae's insistence that he'd come. Resents the self-esteem boost they gave me. Because it makes it suck that much more that my pessimistic, self-deprecating side was right.

My head isn't in the game as I make my rounds, chatting with patrons. Sure, I'm still able to flirt my way into a few private dances, but I'm off tonight.

"Hey girl, you alright?" Drea, one of the bartenders, touches my hand gently as I stop by the bar to grab some drinks.

"Why? Do I not look alright?" I glance down at my black lace bodysuit, my breasts pushed up as high as they can go and the high cut thong showing off my thighs and ass. I picked some of my favorite outfits for tonight, in case Shane came. *Ugh, pathetic.*

She scoffs. "You look incredible, as always. You know that. You just seem a little distracted tonight. And last night, you disappeared in the middle of a set."

"I am a little distracted. Not for the same reason as last night, thankfully. That was bad sushi."

Drea grimaces in sympathy. As a fellow monster, the club owner knows I'm a succubus, but the rest of the staff doesn't. My boss was not happy that she had to use some of her fae magic to alter the memories of everyone who saw me vanish from the stage.

"So if it's not food poisoning again, what's going on?"

Damn, I was hoping she'd let it go. I really need to bring those drinks back. "A...friend said they might come see me."

She quirks a dark eyebrow. "A friend?"

"Yeah. But they probably were too busy. It's fine." I grit my teeth, thankful that the dark club lighting hides the pinking of my cheeks. "Anyway, I better go take these over to the Mr. Important Businessman looking for an innocent girl to impress with his cash before he gets annoyed." I bat my eyelashes at Drea, giving her my best impression of a naïve, wide-eyed girl.

"Have fun, Candy. Don't let his huge wallet intimidate you." Drea winks, and some of my disappointment slides away.

I love this job. People judge strippers and some clubs are a nightmare to work at. But Heaven's Door is nice, the people I work with are supportive, and I make great money. I love the acting, tapping into people's fantasies, and feeling the raw desire thrumming around me. There isn't a better job out there for me that I can think of. I'm not going to let some judgmental nerd I'm inexplicably crushing on ruin my night.

Putting on my best doe-eyed smile, I head back over to the patron and let myself sink into my work.

SHANE

"MAKE A DECISION, DAMMIT!" I curse at myself as I grip the steering wheel and stare over at the neon sign for Heaven's Door. The same sign I've been staring at for almost an hour. Nerves and self-doubt warring with hope and desire. I'm surprised I even made it as far as the club parking lot, with how my mind tortured me all day.

Did she really want me to come, or was she just being polite?

Was she actually flirting with me or was I just reading into everything she said because she's a succubus who oozes sex appeal as a default?

Would it be wrong for me to take her up on her offer after the terrible way we met? Or would it be worse to not show up after I told her I would?

I curse again. Sometimes I wish the universe would give me a sign, so I didn't have to make these sorts of decisions. I'm terrible at reading people. I wouldn't have wandered into a sex cult's summoning ritual otherwise.

Inhaling deeply, I close my eyes and turn on the radio, hoping that some music will calm me enough to decide. The distinctive bass line of "Maneater" greets me, and I cackle in surprise. I asked for a sign and this song literally tells me "watch out boy, she'll chew you up." So then why do I suddenly feel the push to go inside? To embrace my fate of being consumed by the most captivating woman I've ever met.

Fuck it. I know I'll regret this, but I'm out of my car before I can let indecision take over again. Surely I won't be walking into a terrible situation two nights in a row.

My hands shake with nerves as I hand the bouncer the cover charge, almost spilling the over-abundant wad of bills I brought with me all over the floor. I cleaned out a good chunk of my embarrassingly small savings account earlier since I have no clue how much things cost at a strip club. The burly man cocks an eyebrow at my cash and grins. "Have fun, kid."

Part of me wants to protest that I'm almost 25 and not a kid, but arguing with the bouncer sounds like a terrible idea. I nod and shuffle into the dark, neon-soaked club, eyes immediately drawn to the main stage, where a brunette twirls around a pole to Whitesnake, her small perky breasts exposed. I try not to flush at the sight. I've seen naked women before. I saw one last night.

Shit, I shouldn't think about that, or I'll get a boner.

Every fiber of my being wants to cling to the darker booths of the club and hide until I see Elle, but I should grab a drink before I go lurk in the shadows like some nervous weirdo.

The woman behind the bar pushes her cropped black hair behind her ear and plasters on a pleasant smile as I approach. "Hey there! What can I get you?"

"Vodka soda, please. Thank you."

Her mouth quirks into a more genuine smile. "Aren't you a polite one? Sure thing, honey."

As she makes the drink, I scan the room again, heightening my senses with a bit of magic to find Elle. But I don't see her anywhere. Maybe she's not even working tonight, and I misunderstood.

When I turn back to the bartender, she's done with my drink. I tug a clump of bills out of my wallet and pay, too worried to care that I tipped more than the cost of the drink. Her eyes widen for a moment before scooping up the cash, giving me an assessing look.

Oh no, did I already violate some kind of strip club rule by ordering a drink before watching the dancers? Am I not supposed to tip?

"First time?" she asks, a hint of amusement in her tone.

Blood rushes to my face and I grab my drink, taking a hefty swig and coughing at the burn. "Uh, yeah. Sorry."

She grins, the broad smile loosening the knot in my stomach a bit. "Don't apologize, honey. Let me help you out. You here to just watch the dancers or do you want some company? Crystal's a sweetie and I'm sure she'd love to talk to you. But I can tell the girls to let you approach them if you're too shy for talking tonight." She winks at me and refills my glass. I didn't realize I'd already emptied it. "On the house."

"Thank you. I'm, uh, I'm actually here to see someone, but I don't see her, so I'm not sure how long I'll be—"

"Wait. Are *you* the guy Candy's been on edge waiting for?"

My heart skips a beat. *She's been waiting for me?* "Candy?"

"Yeah. Big curly black hair, wicked eyes, tits and ass to die for. And you're...huh." She scans over my face, then down to take in my freshly starched button-down. "I'd never have guessed."

"Um, okay..."

"Sorry! You're just not her usual type."

"Oh." The knot in my stomach comes back with a vengeance. Of course a pasty ginger wouldn't be a succubus' usual type.

"No, don't look like that! Oh honey, that's a *good* thing, I promise." She chuckles and pats my hand.

As the song playing ends, the DJ speaks over the music. "Get those dollar bills ready because coming to the main stage next, we have the sweetest temptation, Candy!"

"Better go grab a seat by the stage before you miss your girl."

I nod and force my shaky legs to take me to one of the open seats along the stage as the DJ blathers about some drink special they've got going. I sit down just as the music changes to a slow, pulsating song.

"Here she is, the one we all want a taste of—Candy!"

My breath catches, and time slows as she slinks onto the stage. Every step is unbearably sensual, her wide hips swaying temptingly in time with the music. In her human form, her luminous rose-tinged white skin stands out against the dark stage. Her abundant breasts are barely contained by a lacy pink bra that reminds me of the shade of her skin when she's in her succubus form. The matching skirt doesn't cover the full curve of her ass as she moves. But what captivates me is her face. Her effortlessly sultry gaze sweeps out over the room as she approaches the pole, taking in the space and drawing everyone's eyes to her.

My palms sweat as she turns in my direction and I know the second she sees me because there's a flash of surprise in her eyes that breaks through the sensuality for a split second. She turns away and dances to the other side of the stage and for an excruciating moment I panic, thinking she's upset that I came.

But then she turns back and moves toward me, her dark gaze boring into me like a predator stalking her prey. I'm trapped by the sight of her as she slides down to her knees when she reaches me, running her hands along her sides and up to cup her breasts. She slides her palms down her thighs, widening her legs and granting me a glimpse of her panties. My cock throbs in my pants and my breath hitches as she runs her fingers up her inner thigh and dangerously close to her covered pussy.

There's a gleam of mischief in her eyes as I scramble to pull out money for her. She moves closer, turning her hip to me so I can reach the g-string peeking out over the top of her skirt. My fingers tremble as I slip the bills under the string, and I do my best to not touch her, but she subtly leans into my hand and smiles at me.

When she speaks, her words are barely audible over the thrumming music and my hammering pulse. "Mmm, you're here. I was getting worried you wouldn't show. But I should've known you'd be a good boy and come for me."

My brows shoot up and my cock aches with need. She giggles, moving away and winking as she dances back to the pole. If I don't get a hold of myself, I'm going to come for her right now.

5

ELLE

When I'm on the stage, I rarely do more than slink around and do an occasional spin around the pole. But seeing the way Shane tracks each of my movements with eager, earnest interest, I can't resist showing off a little. His eyes on me feel so damn good. Even when I'm dancing toward another patron, prickles of excitement dance across my bare skin knowing he's watching.

I tease him, going to another group of men to unwrap my tiny skirt and bare my breasts. It's also a test to see if he's the jealous type. Because I'm not putting up with possessive bullshit. Been there, done that, have the emotional baggage to go along with it. But when I turn back to face Shane, there's only raw desire and a charming, though futile, attempt to suppress the arousal showing in his expression.

I slide down the pole and to the floor, spreading my legs open directly toward him and running my hands up my thighs. Then I roll over and press my hips back in his direction to give him a generous view of my ass. My nipples harden and my clit pulses when I hear his sharp intake of air over the rumbling bass. When I turn over my shoulder to face him, he's placed a neat stack of bills on the stage. His face flushes a deeper red, and he looks down.

Gods, he is too sweet. Why does that make me so hot for him?

By the time my set ends, I'm panting just as much as Shane is, though I do a better job of disguising it. I'm lucky I got off the stage before I soaked through my panties.

My coworker Tiffany raises a brow at me as I head back into the dressing room, flushed and breathless. "You okay?"

"Yeah! Just got into the music. I love that song," I lie. I don't even know the name of the song I danced to. That mattered so little compared to the exhilaration of Shane watching me.

Her plush lips twist into a smirk and she brushes her braids over one shoulder as she bends over to adjust her stocking. "Sure."

She's called onto the stage before she can press me for more. Not that I'd normally care about gossiping about our dances and the patrons. But it feels wrong to do that with Shane since I asked him to come here.

He's waiting for me out there. I grimace as I slip off my damp panties and change back into the black bodysuit I was wearing earlier. That was my last dance for the night, so I'm free to go work out on the floor. Free to talk to him.

I take a moment to compose myself. What I really want to do is rub one out and get some relief, but I'm not about to do that in this cramped dressing room. Despite succubus stereotypes, my lust doesn't control me or cloud my mind more than anyone else's would. It's more like a deep ache or hunger that gnaws at me when unsated. With any luck, I'll get some relief soon.

Fixing my lipstick in the mirror, I roll my shoulders and take a couple of deep breaths. The flutters in my stomach don't go away completely, but they're more manageable.

There's nothing for me to worry about. I flirt with men here all the time. Sure, I don't want to actually screw most patrons, but it's enjoyable and a simple, low effort way to feed my hunger for desire. The thought of being worried about what a shy witch thinks of me —a damn succubus—is laughable. And yet the nerves are still there.

There's something about Shane that calls to a deep-seated instinct in me that goes beyond anything I've experienced before. I knew as soon as I heard him shame those cultists for their actions. No one's ever stood up for me like that. Granted, I've never needed them to—I can take care of myself. But still. It was hot. And as much as I don't want to admit it, it felt good to be taken care of.

It could also be that he seems so innocent and shy, with repressed lust simmering under the surface. It makes sense that would call to me. I want to make him so turned on that he loses control. To completely unmake him and drag him into the darkest depths of desire. How very stereotypical succubus of me.

Man, I wish I had time to call Xae. They'd have some good advice on how to keep that side of me in check. They've got over fifty years of experience on me. Not that they're home right now. They're probably out hooking up with someone. Or multiple someones.

I sigh, checking the mirror and adjusting my tits so they're threatening to fall out of the cups of the bodysuit. *You've got this, Elle. That sexy nerd won't know what hit him.*

My stomach sinks for a moment when I head out into the club and don't see him by the stage. But Drea catches my eye with a smirk and points over to a booth in the corner that seems darker than usual.

I take my time, pushing down another surge of nerves as I wander through the club and chat with a few patrons. A sad-looking man in a rumpled suit opens his mouth to ask me for a dance, but I flit away before he can, calling Missy over. Normally, I'd be happy to play therapist while I straddled a stranger's lap, but not tonight.

By the time I reach the darkened corner where Shane's sitting, I'm practically vibrating with anticipation. He looks up from his drink as my heels click against the floor and his eyes widen, like he wasn't expecting me to come over.

Shane scrambles to his feet, setting down his tumbler so quickly that some of the liquor sloshes over the side. He winces down at it, then gives me a sheepish smile. "El—I mean, uh, Candy!"

"Hello Shane." I smile back at him and step closer, cocking a hip to the side as I take in the well-tailored pants that hug his thighs and the rucked up sleeves of his dress shirt. When his mouth moves wordlessly and his eyes dip down to my breasts, then quickly back up to my face, my smile widens and a fond warmth settles in my chest. "Mind if I sit?"

"Oh! Not at all, please. Can I, uh, would you like a drink?" He steps back from the booth and I slide in past him, letting my hip brush against his.

"I'm good for now. But thanks." He continues to stand there, frozen. "Are you going to join me?"

"Shit, yeah, of course. Gods, I'm acting like a complete weirdo.

I'm so sorry." Shane sits down on the other end of the curved booth, as far away from me as possible.

"I don't bite, you know," I say with a laugh.

"I didn't know what would be appropriate. Plus, I wanted to see your face if we're talking."

"Shane, we're in a strip club. It's okay if you want to be a bit closer." I run a hand idly across the swell of my breasts and grin as he tracks the movement. "And it's okay if you want to look somewhere other than my face."

He coughs, looking away to take a sip of his drink. "Right. Of course. Sorry."

"You've got nothing to apologize for. I appreciate you being respectful. Though I also wouldn't mind if you got a little less courteous." I slide closer to him and his grip on his glass tightens.

"O-oh. Okay, uh…"

A sudden jolt of discomfort hits me. *Shit, am I totally misreading him? Is he nervous or does he not want me that way?*

"Shane, are you interested in me? It's okay if you're not. I appreciate you coming to see me, even if it was just to check and make sure I'm okay after last night. I don't want to make you uncomfortable."

His brows shoot up. "N-no, I'm…I'm interested. Very interested! I'm just…this is new for me and I don't want to do anything inappropriate or assume that you invited me here for anything beyond doing your job. You were beautiful on the stage. That was the most beautiful thing I've ever seen. Not that you're a thing! You're a goddess! I mean, I…I'm going to shut up now." He clears his throat and looks away.

"A goddess, huh? Would you like to worship me, witch?"

"Gods, yes," he sighs, and then looks shocked he said it aloud. "I'd also like to get to know you as a person."

"Oh, yeah?"

"Yeah." Shane smiles and meets my gaze. His warm hazel eyes sparkle with mischief behind his glasses. "It'd help me pay tribute to you more effectively."

A peal of laughter escapes my lips, and he grins back, finally relaxing a hint. "I can't argue with that. What would you like to know?"

"Everything."

I lift a brow. "That might take a while."

He slides a centimeter closer to me, the movement almost imperceptible. "My time is yours if you want it."

My stomach flutters at his choice of words. Offering himself to me, but only if I want to take him. It's far too appealing for me to want to stick with basic chit chat. I slide in closer until my leg touches his and he sucks in a breath, but doesn't move away. I reach up and fiddle with the collar of his shirt, savoring the way his throat works as I do. Damn, he smells good. That same blend of wood-smoke and magic as last night. "What if I want more than just your time?"

"I-I'm yours for whatever you want." A heady blend of arousal and nerves surges from him. It makes me want to grab him and kiss away those nerves. Not that I can do that at work. Not unless...

"Do you want to take me to the champagne room?"

"Huh?" The awed hope in his expression dims. "Oh, right. Yeah. I think I brought enough money...how much does that cost?"

Crap, that sounded like I was telling him I wanted him here so I could make some money off of him. Money is nice, but I want him for more than easy cash.

He digs through his wallet, but I grab his wrist. He freezes. "Shit, is that rude to ask?"

I shake my head and stroke the back of his hand with my

thumb before releasing him. "If it makes you feel better for this to be a transaction, that's fine. But I didn't invite you here to take your money, Shane."

If his eyes could pop out of his head, they would. I suppress a giggle as he gives me a perplexed look. "Are you sure? I...I can pay. Or I'd be happy to just keep talking and get to know you more. I don't need you to, um, entertain me."

"I know I don't *need* to do anything. I *want* to. Though, if it makes things hotter for you, you can pretend to pay me, and I'll give the money back before you leave." The idea sends a thrill through me. I wouldn't mind him using that stack of bills to pretend to coax me to do naughtier and naughtier things. To do things I shouldn't do with a customer. Fuck. I need to get him alone. I'm starving at the thought.

"Oh wow, uh, if you're sure, then—"

I grab his wrist and tug him up out of the booth with me. "Take me to the champagne room. Now."

6

J ust be cool. Relax. Yes, the most singularly attractive creature
you've ever been around is taking you into a room to be alone.
Yes, against all odds, she's been fucking you with her eyes and it
wasn't to get your money. But be chill. And for the love of the
gods, don't come in your damn pants.

"This is...nice. Are those mirrors on the walls?" *Real smooth.* Of
course there are mirrors on the walls. This is a room where people
go to watch a girl get naked and get private lap dances. I don't
think more than that happens, but how the hell would I know?
"They're not one-way mirrors, are they? For people to monitor us?"

Elle motions for me to sit on a leather bench seat against the
far wall, smiling at me as she shuts the door behind her. The club

music fades to a low thrum, making the beating of my heart that much louder in my head. "Nope, just regular mirrors." She glances up at a small camera hidden in the corner. "We use those to make sure everyone stays safe in here. That and the doors don't lock. But if you're shy, you can use some of your magic to obscure us. I think I can handle you without supervision. You'll be a good boy for me, won't you?"

My fingers tighten in the fabric of my pants, nails digging into my legs to keep some semblance of control as my cock swells. *Yes, I'll be so good for you.* "I...yes."

"Do you want me to dance for you? Show you more than I could out there?" Elle moves to a stereo set into the wall and sensual, thumping music plays. She walks over to a tiny stage in the center of the room and steps up onto it, leisurely moving around the pole until she loops around to lock eyes with me.

"If you want to. Or we could keep talking!"

A slight frown twists her full lips, and she steps off the stage, closing the distance between us. "Is that what you want? To keep talking?" She leans over me, her mouth brushing against my ear as she whispers. "Or do you want more?"

I don't know what the right answer is. Honestly, I want to know everything about Elle, so talking would be great. And with talking, there's a much smaller chance of me embarrassing myself the second she gets close, like the inexperienced virgin I am. The only person who's ever gone near my cock other than me was my college girlfriend. And that was only when she tried to give me a hand job as an apology for cheating on me. Needless to say, I didn't let her.

It's not that I don't want sex. Trust me, I do. It just hasn't happened. With school, magical pursuits, and trying to build my PI business, I haven't given myself the chance to find someone to have sex with. And now I have a succubus offering to do gods know what with me. Fuck, why didn't I just go out and try to sleep with random people? I should've at least jacked off before I came here. I'm such an idiot.

She leans back and looks down at me, casually sliding her hand up the side of my thigh as she waits for my answer. Words tumble out of my mouth unbidden. "I want more. I want to know you. I want to take you out for coffee and find out about your dreams. I want to go to dinner and discuss our deepest secrets, then order your favorite dessert. I want to taste it on your tongue and then take you home and see if it's anywhere as sweet as your pussy, though I know it won't be." *Where the fuck did that come from?* "So, uh, yeah. I want more," I add with an awkward laugh.

There's a long pause as her eyes flare with an emotion I can't read. Probably pity or regret for bringing me in here. I duck my head, unable to bear the embarrassing rejection coming my way, but her hand darts out to grab my chin and tilts it back up to look at her.

"I like the sound of all of that, sweet witch. But, for tonight, why don't we start with a lap dance?"

"W-what?" I blink up at her, my brain no longer functioning. She likes the sound of that? Am I dreaming or in some kind of alternate universe? Maybe they sacrificed me at that coven ritual, and this is all just a hallucination of my dying brain. At least it's a pleasant way to go.

"I'd like to give you a lap dance. It's a little late for coffee." She winks at me, rubbing my thigh again with teasing light strokes.

"That'd be nice. Th-thanks!" My voice breaks slightly and she raises a brow.

"You sure?"

Get your shit together! I speak more confidently this time, my voice a low rasp I barely recognize. "Yeah. As long as you agree to get that coffee with me sometime soon."

She lets out a peal of bubbly laughter. The sound fizzes through me, more intoxicating than any champagne served in this room. "You drive a hard bargain." Her eyes dip down to my lap and she licks her lips as she eyes the prominent bulge there. "Deal."

Without warning, she moves away and my body screams to grab her and pull her back to me. To kiss her and taste her skin, trailing my way down her body and worshiping every inch of her lush form.

She grabs a business card for the club sitting on top of the stereo and scribbles something on the back. Then she's back in front of me, bending over and slipping the card into my pocket. I let out a choked sound when her fingers brush against my cock through the fabric of my pants.

"My number. Don't want to get carried away and forget to give it to you before you leave. Promise you'll call me, witch. Breaking deals with a demon is a bad idea."

Her husky warning sends a shiver down my spine. "I promise."

Elle grins down at me with gleaming hunger in her eyes. "Good boy. Now keep your hands on the couch and don't move them unless I tell you to."

I nod, swallowing hard as I grab onto the couch. She closes her eyes for a moment, feeling the music as she runs her hands up her sides, fingertips trailing against her soft stomach and then up to her breasts. She turns to face away, giving me a perfect view of her full, rounded ass in the thin lace bodysuit, then peels the bodysuit the rest of the way off. There's an even tinier g-string underneath, and she hooks her fingers in it for a teasing moment, but doesn't take it off.

Elle turns around and my mouth goes dry. I've already seen her topless, both in her human and monster forms, but it still over-whelms me. Her breasts would more than fill my hands, full teardrops tipped with rosy pink nipples that stiffen under my gaze. I've always loved breasts—big, small, and everything in between. But gods, hers are perfection.

Her pale skin flushes a deeper pink as she closes the distance between us, like her succubus form is peeking through. It makes me wonder... "I can cover the camera."

She pauses as she leans over to rest her hands on my thighs. "Oh? What do you think is going to happen that we'd need to hide?"

I can't tell if she's teasing me or worried I expect more than just a dance from her. "In case you want to shift to your other form." Her lip twitches, and I hurry to elaborate. "You're beautiful both ways! Either way is perfect. Just, uh, if that makes you more comfortable. Gods, why can't I stop talking? You're here in front of me, looking like *that,* and I can't keep my mouth shut."

Elle giggles again, and her breasts shake enticingly with the movement. "You can talk as much as you want, Shane." She strad-dles me, her knees on either side of my legs, bringing her breasts directly in front of my face. "If you're lucky, I'll give you something else to do with your mouth soon."

"Oh, fuck." I gasp as she sinks down to rest her weight on my lap, the warm heat of her covered pussy resting right on top of my straining erection. My grip on the couch tightens as she threads a hand through my hair, tugging my head back with a slight prick of pain to look into her eyes.

"Mmm, is that for me?" She rolls her hips, grinding down against me in a slow, undulating tease.

"Y-yes." I can barely choke out the words, all the blood in my body shooting straight to my dick.

"How long has that big, hard cock been aching for me?" Elle whispers, leaning in to press her lips to my throat as she rocks herself against me again.

"Since the moment I saw you last night." Fuck. I shouldn't have said that.

"Oh? So why didn't you want me to sate your urges like the rest of that coven? I was there, trapped and at your mercy. You could have made me do anything you wanted."

My cheeks heat with indignation, and my cock softens slightly. "I don't take anything that's not given with consent."

She frowns, but rolls her hips against me again. "But I'm a succubus. Doesn't that mean I'm obliged to indulge and feast on others' desires?"

I grab her hips to keep her still. "I don't care what you are— what they wanted to do was rape. I would never...they're disgusting."

Elle stares down at me, emotion flickering over her face. "You really are good, aren't you? It's not an act."

"I don't feel very good, coming here and taking advantage of your kindness tonight. I shouldn't have...you don't have to do this. You don't owe me anything for last night."

"Shane..." She bites her lower lip and looks down.

"I'm sorry, Elle. I'll go—"

"I told you to keep your hands on the couch."

"W-what?"

"Your hands are touching me, witch."

"I'm sorry! I didn't mean to." I immediately release her hips and she stands. Guess that answers that question—she was just doing this as a favor.

Just as I'm about to stand and spew out a stream of more apologies, she turns and sits back down on my lap, leaning back against my chest as she circles her ass against me. I move to grip the couch again like she told me to, but she grabs my hands and brings them up to cup her breasts. My cock surges back to life and I let out a shuddering breath, so confused and turned on.

She guides me to knead her tits and grinds on me again, a small breathy gasp escaping her lips as my thumb brushes her nipple. "Are you going to behave? Or do I have to tie your hands up?"

I inhale sharply at the thought of being tied up and completely at her mercy. "I-I'll do whatever you want me to do, Elle."

She grins back at me over her shoulder, then slides one of my hands down to her panties, using my fingers to push the—*oh fuck, very damp fabric*—to the side. "Use your magic to cover the camera."

Stumbling over the words of the simple incantation that will obscure us from view, I nod when it's done.

Elle sighs and guides my fingers to her pussy and my balls tighten, cock throbbing at the sensation. It feels like a fever dream that I'm touching her. "I've thought about you since last night, too. And I've been wet since you got here."

My brain finally allows me to believe her, feeling just how wet she is and hearing the husky need in her voice.

"Make me come."

Those three words are all I need. I may not have ever touched a woman before, but I'll be damned if I don't find a way to do as she commands.

7

ELLE

The moment Shane's fingers glide across my pussy, I gasp. The nervous arousal radiating off of him is so potent it makes my head spin. But when his fingers don't move again, I let out a frustrated sigh. What is he waiting for? He better not think he's going to tease me, because if I don't come in the next few minutes, I think I'll die. Or at least pass out from the need to sate my hunger.

"Did you not hear me? *Touch me.*"

Shane gasps, but still hesitates. "Can you show me what you like? I've never—uh, I mean, I know everyone is different and I want to make you feel good."

I'm glad I'm turned away because his earnest words make me

grin like a fool. When was the last time someone asked me what I wanted and didn't just assume I'd get off without effort because of what I am?

Placing my hand back on top of his, I guide two of his fingers down to gather up some of my wetness, then slide them up to my clit. "Roll my clit with your fingers. Not directly on it, but on the sides."

I can feel him nod behind me and then tentatively move his fingers around my clit. "A little more pressure—" Sparks of pleasure sizzle through me as he follows my command. "Ahh, yes. Like that. Don't stop or change what you're doing unless I tell you to."

His cock jolts against my ass, and he groans under his breath. "Y-yes." If I didn't know any better, I'd think he was the succubus by how he seems to get off on my pleasure.

Rocking my hips into his touch, my orgasm builds quickly. The hand on my breast tightens when I moan.

"Please. I know you said not to move my hands unless you told me to, but I need—"

"Play with my breasts. Pinch my nipples." I gasp when he exhales a shaky "thank you" and immediately obeys.

As soon as he does, I know I'm lost. "Keep doing that. Oh gods, yes. That's it, just like that—fuck!" My orgasm slams into me and I writhe in his lap, rolling my hips against his fingers, which diligently stroke me exactly how I instructed through the whole thing.

Shane gasps and another wave of release washes over me, turning me into a shaking mess. I remove his hand from my pussy when I can't take it any longer and move off of his lap, sinking down to my knees in front of him. I'm sated, but want to get my hands on him and give him pleasure like he did for me.

"You did so well, sweet witch. Now let me reward you for being so good."

His mouth parts as he breathes heavily, eyes widening. A moment later, his hands dart down to his crotch to cover it. "I-I'm good."

"The way your thick cock rubbed against my ass tells me otherwise. I want to, Shane. Not because I think I owe you something. I *want* to."

His expression becomes pained, and his breath stutters. "I–I don't, it's not—"

I've never had this reaction before. It's hard for my ego not to feel a little bruised. But I can sense his arousal dimming as he starts to panic. "It's okay. If you don't want me to, I won't."

"I do, oh gods, this is so fucking humiliating." He winces. "I, uh, I already came. You just sounded so good, and it was amazing to touch you and feel you against me."

No wonder my orgasm was so intense—I was experiencing his as well. I place a hand on his thigh and squeeze. "You enjoyed touching me that much?"

"Yes. I'd do it over and over, if you'd let me." His eyes glimmer down at me with earnest desire, cheeks pink as his glasses slide down his nose to give him a deliciously flustered look.

"Mmm, I like the sound of that, so I'll let it slide this time. But from now on, you'll be a good little witch and ask for my permission to come."

His eyes flare with interest, and I taste his excitement on my tongue. "O-okay."

Gods, he's a delight. I'm tempted to tease him until he's hard again and see how long he lasts before he's begging me to come. But I need to get back to work.

"You okay to go back out there, or should I get you something to clean up with?" I ask with a smirk down at his crotch. "Oh, I know! I'll go get your shirt I borrowed and you can hold it in front of the wet spot."

He grimaces, but laughs. "I'll be okay. It should be dark enough and, uh, I like the idea of you keeping my shirt."

"Oh, do you?" A foolish grin creeps across my face and my heart flutters with something I haven't felt in a very long time. *Affection.* I'm not just horny for Shane. I think I might *like* him.

"Yeah, it looked much better on you."

"Well, good. Because I didn't want to give up my new favorite sleep shirt."

His eyes widen. "You slept in it?"

I shrug and try not to blush. *Why did I tell him that?* "It smelled good."

A slow smile stretches across his face. "You like the way I smell?"

Should I be coy or just tell him how I feel? Some guys get scared away if you come on too strong, but he literally told me he wanted to know everything about me, so I choose to be honest. "I like everything about you. I mean, no one's perfect and I'm not saying we should run off and get married, but I like you. Something in my gut tells me you're special."

Shane huffs out a shocked laugh. "I'm nothing special. But I won't argue with you if it means I get to see you again."

"Of course you're seeing me again! You made a deal with me for coffee."

"True, I don't want you to drag me to hell and torture me if I break our agreement."

"I don't know...I get the feeling you might enjoy my brand of torture."

He looks toward the door, clearing his throat in an attempt to cover his blush at my words. "I should let you get back to work."

I don't want to stop talking now that he's finally relaxing around me and believes that my interest is genuine, but he's right. "Yeah, I'm already on thin ice for disappearing last night."

"I meant to ask, how the hell did you explain that? It looked like you were in the middle of a dance when you showed up in the summoning circle."

"The owner of the club is a monster, too. A fae. She had to use magic to alter the memories of the non-paranormals that saw it. That takes a lot of effort, so she's not too happy with me."

Shane shakes his head in sympathy. "Oof, yeah, don't want to piss off a fae. I'll head out and let you work."

We walk to the door, but Shane pauses as he goes to open it. "Thank you, Elle. I never imagined I'd be walking out of here with a coffee date lined up with the loveliest person I've ever met."

The fluttering revs up again in my chest. People compliment me a lot—it's part of being a succubus and a stripper. But this seems so sincere. Like he expects nothing in return for his kindness. "I bet you didn't expect to walk out with jizz in your pants, either."

Most guys wouldn't like me teasing, but he just laughs right along with me. "No, that felt like a forgone conclusion."

Before I can stop myself, I lean in and kiss him lightly. He freezes for a second, but then he's kissing me back with aching tenderness. Neither one of us deepens the kiss, but we're both breathless and flushed when our mouths part.

"Good night, Shane."

He opens the door and looks back at me one last time. "Good night, Elle. Or shit, I mean, Candy. Have a good rest of your shift."

Shane slinks into the shadows of the club, no doubt using magic to cover his exit so no one sees his wet pants. With a smile, I head back to work, knowing that he'll be on my mind as I flirt and charm my way through the club for the rest of the night.

8

"A dark laugh breaks through the eerie silence of the cavern. Ghostly blue lanterns flare to life around you as the laugh gets louder, echoing off the damp stone walls until it becomes earsplitting. As suddenly as it began, it ceases and a cloaked figure appears before your party. 'You shouldn't have come here, foolish mortals.'"

"I take out my greataxe and charge toward the lich!"

My eyebrow quirks. Typical Stacy, charging into the fight with no plan.

Everyone else at the table groans. Mark throws his character sheet down onto the table in frustration, scattering dice in its wake. "What? No! Come on! I was going to try to talk to it first.

You're going to get us all killed again!"

Stacy scowls back at him through the curtain of her long blonde hair, her fawn cheeks reddening as her anger builds. "But it's what Graxlar would do!"

"Oh yeah? Well, maybe Dresh should polymorph Graxlar into a toad, because that's what *he* would do."

I watch from behind the Dungeon Master screen as they break out into an argument. When Mark and Stacy go at it, there's no stopping them. I mentally yell at them both to quit their nonsense, but don't say anything aloud. I don't want to do anything to jeopardize the few friendships I've made with paranormals in the city, let alone ones that have similar interests to me.

Unfortunately, their argument shows no sign of ending. "Uh, guess we'll stop there for tonight..."

Nathan shoots me a sympathetic glance, then rolls his eyes at the arguing pair as I start to clean up my stuff. They're inches from each other's faces and they look like they're about to break out into a fistfight or make out on top of the table. "You guys should just fuck and get it over with already," he mutters.

Stacy flips him off, but Mark's olive cheeks darken and he shakes his head, turning to glare at Nathan. "Not cool, man. You wouldn't say shit like that to us if we were both guys. Stacy doesn't need your misogynist crap."

Nathan glares at him. "Yes, I would! I'm not a misogynist. If you and Shane were acting like sexually repressed morons, I'd tell you to go blow each other."

Stacy scoffs. "You're just jealous that no one will touch your nasty wolf dick, Nathan. Don't project onto others."

I hold my hands up, trying to calm everyone down. "That's enough. Stacy and Mark, stop arguing at the table. Nathan, stop harassing Stacy and Mark about their personal lives. Stacy, don't bring Nathan's dick into this. And everyone, remember this is just a game where we roll dice. It's supposed to be fun!"

The three of them give me a chorus of sheepish apologies, and Nathan turns to the other two. "Sorry. That was messed up of me to say. I just want you both to be happy, but it's none of my business."

Stacy frowns apologetically. "Sorry I said your wolf dick was nasty. I'm sure it's totally fine." Mark gives him a curt nod. Neither of them acknowledge their fight, not even looking at each other as they pack up and head out separately.

Nathan shakes his head as he helps me clean up the mess of snacks and soda cans. "Sorry, Shane. I shouldn't have said anything. It's just, I know how hard you worked planning that lich fight and we don't get a lot of opportunities to play."

"No worries, man." I consider the dark circles under his eyes and the gray tinge to his dark brown skin. "It's getting close to the full moon, isn't it? Is the charm I gave you still working?"

Nathan and I met during my first PI gig in the city, and became friends after we realized we both play D&D. A month ago, I helped him with an enchanted pendant that would control his shifting, because his transformations during the full moon were brutal after his ex broke up with him. Unfortunately, suppressing shifting can have negative effects.

He sighs. "Yeah. Still doesn't excuse me being a dick. If I could just get out of my head and get laid, I could stop using the charm. But I'm still not over Vanessa, so..."

"You don't have to explain yourself to me. She broke your heart. It's okay to not be over that."

Nathan claps a firm hand on my shoulder. "Thanks man. If you ever have any girl troubles, I'm here for you, too." He pauses. "Or guy troubles! I, uh, shit. I guess I've never heard you mention someone, so I have no clue what you're into."

My cheeks heat. I've never had a friend close enough to talk to about my sexuality or love life, but maybe Nathan and I are closer than I realized. He doesn't seem like the kind of guy who'd judge me, but my gut still clenches with nerves before I reply. "I'm, uh... I'm into both. Just haven't had much experience with either."

Nathan takes my answer in stride. "Ah, okay. Cool. I mean, not cool that you haven't had any experience if you'd like some. I'd offer to suck your dick, but I'm not really into dudes."

"I don't—that's not—"

He squeezes my shoulder and chuckles. "Relax, witch. I'm messing with you."

I huff out an embarrassed laugh, my mind immediately going to Elle when he called me witch. "I, um, I did meet someone the other night. I don't think anything will happen though—she told me to call her, but she hasn't returned my call after I left her a message."

"Ah damn, that sucks. Maybe she's just been busy? I know they say to play it cool, but if you like her, I'd try calling again just in case."

"That wouldn't be bothering her? I don't want her to think I'm going to harass her into going on a date." Even though she made me swear to go on one with her.

"A second call is okay. If she doesn't answer or call back, then you'll know to leave her alone."

My pulse races at the thought of calling her again. Gods, I haven't been able to stop thinking about her. My eyes dart over to the phone and Nathan chuckles. "Do you want me to stay for moral support?"

"N-no! I'm good."

He laughs again. "Alright. Good luck! Let me know next game night how it goes—that is, if Stacy and Mark haven't murdered each other before then."

I walk Nathan to the door of my apartment and wave goodbye as he heads down the short hallway to the elevator. When I make my way back into the kitchen and living area of my small place, the sight of the phone makes my palms sweat.

Okay, you can do this. Just pick up the phone and call her. If she's not there, you can just hang up. If she's changed her mind, you'll survive. With shaking hands, I dial the number on the back of the card she gave me and wait breathlessly as the phone rings.

On the third ring, she picks up, and my heart leaps up into my throat.

"Hello?"

"El–" I choke on my words and clear my throat. "Elle? Hi, it's Shane."

"Oh! Shane!" Her voice doesn't sound annoyed or upset. Instead, she sounds...*excited?*

"Y-yeah, I'm sorry to call again like this. I just didn't want you to think I'd forgotten about coffee. But I totally understand if you changed your mind or you don't want—"

"I'm so glad you called again! You didn't leave your number last time."

"I didn't?"

"Nope," she laughs, and the sound sends warmth bubbling through my chest. "It was such a lovely message, but in all your sweet words, you didn't tell me how to call you back."

"Shit, I'm sorry!"

"Mmm, I'll forgive you if you tell me your number now. And have coffee with me tomorrow. I've been waiting for days and I'm very thirsty."

"T-tomorrow works!" I rattle off my number so quickly that she has to tell me to slow down and say it again.

She gives me her address and I scramble for a pen and paper to jot it down. "Pick me up at 10? Unless you have work."

"No! I mean, I have a job, but I set my schedule. So 10 works. Any time you want works, really. Just as long as I get to see you again and this conversation isn't a figment of my imagination."

"I'd think it'd be a lot dirtier of a conversation if it was coming from your imagination, don't you?" Her voice deepens to a sinfully low purr that makes my dick twitch.

"I mean, uh, maybe."

"Maybe? You haven't spent the past few days wondering what it'd be like to put your cock inside me? Because I certainly have thought about how good you'd feel. I've even touched myself while I did."

"Oh gods, really? I...wow."

She laughs. "Really. You're telling me you didn't?"

"I didn't say that. Shit, I hope that's okay and doesn't make me sound like a total creep that only wants you for your body. I'm just drawn to you. Beyond the whole succubus desire magic thing. You're so confident and charming and lovely, and..."

"Gods, you're too sweet. A girl could get used to talking to you. Don't worry, though. You're allowed to want me for both my body and my mind. They're a package deal, after all." She laughs again. "Besides, you wouldn't judge me for wanting your body and not just your mind."

"You want my body?" I sputter out the question.

"Yes, Shane." She says it so matter of fact. I know I'm not unattractive, but she could literally have anyone in her bed. That she wants my skinny, pale ass boggles my mind. "I want your body. I want your beautiful eyes looking at me, your soft lips on my skin, and your strong hands gripping my hips. Most of all, I want that thick cock I saw trapped in your pants. Now stop asking questions you already know the answer to."

My cock swells, leaking pre-cum from the tip onto my boxer briefs. Gods, I can't believe this is real, but who am I to argue? "Yes. Okay, sorry, I won't."

"Good boy. Now, it's late, so I should let you go, shouldn't I?"

"You don't have to..."

"It's okay! I don't want to *keep you up*." She emphasizes the last few words, like she knows just how up and fully at attention my cock is now. "I'll see you tomorrow morning. Sweet dreams, Shane."

"Goodnight, Elle."

I hang up the phone and let out a shocked laugh. I have a coffee date tomorrow. With a gorgeous succubus. Who just told me she's touched herself thinking about me and wants my body.

Fuck. I need to figure out how to keep my dick under control around her. It's late, but I head to the bookshelf in my living room where I have a bunch of dusty old tomes. One of them must have a spell or something that will help me keep from making a fool of myself again.

9

ELLE

"Who was that?" Xae peers up at me over their glass of wine from their seat on the couch as I hang up the phone. They came over for dinner, but that devolved into us gossiping about our other cousins' love lives. I still can't believe Ilyxia ran off with a married changeling she met a week ago. She always was the most reckless of our cousins, but fucking someone who's married is beneath even her.

I can't keep the grin off my face as I rejoin them in the living room and plop down on the chair across from them. "It was the witch I told you about. The one who I invited to the club. Shane." My skin still tingles with a mixture of arousal and anticipation for tomorrow after speaking with him.

Their crimson eyes light up and they clap their hands together. "It was?! Oh, that's amazing, Elle!"

It really is. I know next to nothing about Shane, but I can't help feeling like this is the start of something really special. Maybe it's just my hopeless romantic side finally peeking its head back out after years of hiding away.

They grin at me as their long red tail lashes out to smack my leg playfully. "Look at you! You're glowing. What did he say?"

"He wanted to ask me out for coffee. He called the other day, but didn't leave his number. I still have his message saved—it was so adorable. Gods, I think I really like him, Xae. He's been so sweet and respectful and...this might sound bad, but he's shy and that makes me want to bring out his desires even more."

"No, I get it. Teasing that side out of someone and seeing them finally give in is delicious. Shit, this is exciting! You deserve someone who treats you like a queen."

I grin back at them. "I do, don't I?"

"That's the spirit! Now, tell me everything you know about him."

I proceed to do just that, describing every minute detail I've noticed, from the soft dotting of freckles on his cheeks that grows more prominent when he flushes to the breathy hitch in his voice whenever I say something suggestive. About how he's a witch who uses cloaking magic. How he's so damn sweet and respectful, but has flashes of passion that make me excited to see more.

I leave out the part where he came in his pants—Xae wouldn't judge, but I don't want to betray his trust by blabbing about something that's typically seen as embarrassing. Though, I don't see it that way. It's flattering that he enjoyed touching me that much. Even as a succubus, most people don't care much about my pleasure.

By the time I'm done, Xae has a dreamy look in their eyes. "He sounds perfect for you, Elle. I know I should be warning you about not falling too fast or waiting to see if he's as nice as he seems, but fuck that. Trust your instincts—you've ignored them in the past and look where that got you. No offense."

"No, you're right." I've ended up heartbroken and with a whole closetful of emotional baggage from not trusting my instincts. From letting the potent desires of those around me guide my choices, rather than following my own. With Shane, it's the first time I'm certain that I want someone regardless of if they want me. It's terrifying and exhilarating.

"So, what are you going to wear?"

I grin, thinking of the perfect dress for the occasion. Something cute and floral, but low-cut enough that it'll tempt him into looking at my breasts. I may even forgo panties if I'm feeling wicked.

SHANE

I SHOVE my hand through my hair, checking my reflection in the rearview mirror before getting out of the car. Shit, I hope she doesn't notice the prominent dark circles under my eyes. Last night it took me until 3 am scouring my magic books to find a spell that could help with my problem. Then another hour to gather the components and cast it. I woke up at 9, scrambled to make myself presentable while ignoring my throbbing headache from lack of sleep, and raced out the door so I wouldn't be late picking Elle up.

I didn't even have time to test the spell. For all I know, it'll make my dick shrivel up and fall off. Note to self: Don't cast untested dick magic at 4 am. Or ever.

Gods, I'm such an idiot.

Elle lives in a brick townhouse in a much nicer part of the city than my mediocre apartment. A woman pushing a stroller waves at me as I head down the sun-dappled sidewalk lined with blooming trees. Every step closer to her house makes my heart pound faster. I have to grip the overpriced bouquet I picked up from the florist across the street from my place tighter so it won't slip out of my sweaty palm.

I saw a flash of rosy pink petals as I headed out to my car and thought it was a sign. Standing here on her stoop, ringing the doorbell as I force myself to breathe, I feel like a fool. People don't bring flowers on a first date! Especially when you're just going to get coffee. My eyes dart around for somewhere to abandon the bouquet, but the door swings open before I can ditch it.

"Shane! You're right on time."

Before me, Elle is a vision that makes any thoughts of the bouquet melt away. Her dark curls are pinned up, showing off the delicate curve of her neck and the off-the-shoulder floral dress that dips down over the swell of her lush breasts. My eyes linger there for a second too long before shooting back up to her face, where I'm greeted by her radiant smile.

"Elle! Hello! Gods, you look beautiful."

Her eyes sparkle in amusement at my blurted compliment. "Thank you. You look good, too." She touches my arm in a casual way that still makes my skin sizzle under the fabric of my shirt, then looks down at the bouquet. "Are those for me? How sweet, they're lovely! And they match my dress!"

I glance back down at her dress and indeed the pink roses are the exact shade of the flowers on her dress. My eyes threaten to get caught on her breasts again, but I manage to look back up.

"Come on in. I need to grab my purse and put on some shoes." She wiggles her bare foot at me, which is just as pretty as the rest of her. Her toenails are painted a sparkly green that matches the vines in her dress.

I follow her inside, down a narrow hallway that branches off into a sunroom and an office, past a set of stairs to her living room and kitchen area. Everything is decorated in warm colors that remind me of a sunset, just as elegant and intriguing as the woman who lives here. I do my best to soak in every minor detail of her place, but my eyes keep drawing back to the curve of her hips.

She grabs her purse from the counter, then heads back toward the stairs, where she pauses. "Speaking of shoes, did you want to walk to the coffee shop? It's only a few blocks away and I wouldn't mind the extra time outside during this surprise warm weather."

"Sure, I'm happy to walk."

Elle nods and starts up the stairs. I hesitate, unsure if I should follow. She turns over her shoulder and smiles at me. "I promise I don't have anything scary up here. Well, other than my disaster of a closet."

I trail after her, trying—and failing—not to stare at her ass as I do. She heads into a sunny bedroom with pale green walls and a large four-poster bed. I hover in the doorframe, my courage failing me. Elle goes into a walk-in closet and starts rummaging around.

While she's looking for shoes, I scan the soft and inviting room. It's not at all what I'd think of when imagining the bedroom of a succubus. That is until I notice the mirror over the bed and the large glass cabinet filled with all kinds of...*oh wow*. My face flames as I tear my eyes away from the assortment of sex toys.

My cock swells as I notice more and more subtle, sensual

details around the room—anchor points on the walls, a bench at the foot of the bed which has a cage-like bottom, a row of neatly organized floggers hidden partially behind her vanity. Shit, guess that spell didn't work. I need to think about something else. Something that won't give me a hard-on five minutes into our first date.

"Uh, the weather has been nice, hasn't it? Though I hear it's supposed to get chilly next week. Which is good because short sleeves the week before Halloween feels wrong."

"True!" Elle emerges from her closet with a pair of flats and sits on the bench to slide them on. "I love fall. It's my favorite time of the year. The leaves turning and pumpkin patches. The thinning of the veil between this world and the spirit realm. Oh! Do you do anything special to celebrate Samhain?"

"Not since I moved here. I haven't found a coven yet. Well, I found one, but you know how that turned out. I'll probably just do something small on my own."

Great. If she wasn't already aware of how much of a loser you are, telling her you'll be alone on one of the biggest party nights for the paranormal community certainly gets the message across.

"Speaking of that coven, I'm going to get in touch with the city's paranormal council. If that's okay with you. I can't in good conscience let them go around fucking with other monsters and pretending it's okay."

Elle stands and smooths out her dress, giving me a perplexed look. "You'd do that?"

"Yeah, of course. I should've done it right away, but didn't want to do anything without checking in with you first."

She shrugs. "I didn't even think about reporting it. Stuff like that happens all the time to succubi, so it felt par for the course."

I step into the room and reach out to touch her arm on instinct, hearing the resignation in her voice. "Just because it's a common occurrence doesn't make it right, Elle."

She looks down at where my hand touches her bare skin like she feels the same tingling awareness that I do at the contact, then up into my eyes. "No, I suppose you're right. Thank you, Shane."

Neither one of us moves, lingering close enough to feel the heat between our bodies. "You don't have to thank me."

"I know I don't have to. Still, it means a lot to me." She steps in closer until we're just shy of pressing together. Her violet eyes gleam up at me, daring me to do something.

Like the coward I am, I change the subject. "Do you have any plans for Halloween?"

The tension breaks, and she moves past me, heading back toward the stairs. "My cousin Xae has a big party every year that I usually go to. But that usually just devolves into an orgy fifteen minutes in, and I don't know if I'm in the mood for that this year."

"Oh! Yeah, I could see how that might be tiring."

Elle turns when she reaches the base of the stairs, a mischievous grin on her face. "Have you been to many orgies, Shane?"

"N-no! Other than the failed attempt the other night, no. Why? Is that something you'd want me to do? Because I'm willing to try. I'd try anything for you." She raises a brow. "That is, uh, if this coffee date goes well and you want to see more of me. I'm not assuming that you want to have sex with me!"

"Oh, I definitely do," she purrs, making my traitorous dick harden despite the spell I worked on all night.

"R-right."

"You're adorable when you blush. Did you know that?"

My cheeks grow even warmer at her compliment. "I...I didn't."

"Makes me think about how much fun I'll have teasing you

with more than words." She winks and heads toward the front door, giving me a moment to readjust my dick before we leave.

10

I lazily trace the rim of my empty mug with a finger as I gaze across the cafe table. Shane smiles shyly and rubs the back of his neck as the moment of silence in our conversation stretches between us. I bask in the tension, my pulse thrumming as I wonder where this morning will take us.

So far, the date's been delightful. He insisted on getting my coffee and a variety of pastries, "just in case I got hungry", then pulled my chair out for me like a gentleman. It took a few minutes for him to warm up, but now he's much more confident when he speaks. I've enjoyed drawing him out of his shell and finding that inside is a smart, quirky, and funny man. I'm tempted to end the conversation and ask him back to my place, but the more we talk, the more interested I am in finding out more about the witch sitting across from me.

We've gone over all the general get to know you questions— where did you grow up, how old are you, what's your favorite color, etc. He grew up in a suburb a few states to the north, while I split my childhood between my mom's place in the demon realm and my uncle's condo in the city. Shane's face filled with wonder as he asked me about the demon realm, seeming in no way put off by my description of the hot, craggy landscape and dark spires of my mother's lair. I didn't mention her cabal of eager sex servants and multitude of partners. I'll save that for when he meets the family.

I really shouldn't plan that far ahead. We've barely just met. Even though he's enthusiastic about getting to know me and doesn't seem like the commitment-phobic type, he's young—24 to my 37. Not that the age gap really matters with paranormals like us, our lives stretching significantly longer than humans, but it's still something that made him blush.

I need to stop getting ahead of myself and focus on the present. Focus on the adorable witch currently worrying his lower lip between his teeth, no doubt concerned about filling the lull in our conversation. I could take pity on him and ask another harmless first date question, but I enjoy seeing him squirm a bit. Plus, I can sense he wants to delve deeper, but something is holding him back.

Eventually, he breaks the silence. "Do you like working at the club? Is that what you see yourself doing for the rest of your career?" Shane pauses, then shakes his head. "Not that I'm saying you should want to do something else! If that makes you happy, that's awesome."

I grin back at his endearing addendum. "I love it! Does it suck sometimes? Yeah. People can be assholes and it's hard on my body.

No job is perfect. But it pays well, and it feeds my soul—both figuratively and literally."

"Oh wow, I hadn't even considered the benefits to your succubus side. That's so smart! Plenty of horny humans to feed off of as they pay you for the privilege."

"Exactly! It's refreshing to hear that you understand." I leave the part about other dates being less open-minded unsaid. Every other potential partner I've had assumed that I'd stop stripping and do something more "respectable" once I was in a relationship.

He must understand the meaning behind my words, though. He's very perceptive, beneath all the shy smiles and sweetness. "You're lucky to have found something so fulfilling. Few people have that." Shane smiles back, his earnest expression making my chest squeeze.

"Thank you. I know that I'll stop at some point in the next couple of years, mostly because the hours and physical stress will get old. My dream is to have enough saved by that point to cover most of my expenses and find a part-time job just to keep me busy. I got my degree in clinical psychology, but ended up not finding it a great match for me." I hesitate, unsure if I should tell him about the other major part of my dream life so soon. I don't want to scare him away, so I ease into it. "I'd like to have a cozy home, a dog or a cat, and a partner. Very boring for a sex demon, I know."

He laughs, the sound warm and raspy. "I don't think you could be boring even if you tried. Besides, that sounds perfect."

"What about you? What do you dream of, Shane?" I lean forward, delighting in the way his throat bobs at my suggestive tone and the dip of my dress that shows off more cleavage.

"I, uh, I'm trying to get my PI business off the ground. The nice thing about the paranormal community is that once you do good work for one person, you'll get more business via word of mouth.

But beyond that, I want what you want. I'm not very exciting either." He chuckles to himself, then looks down at his hands. "I want the partner, the pet, the house...and I, um, I want a family."

My breath catches. "You want kids?" No one I've dated had any interest in children. My awful ex laughed at me when I brought it up. *"You? A mother? Gods, Elle, you'd have to stop being such a dirty slut, and we both know you'd never be able to do that."* He'd said it as a way of coming on to me, following it up by grabbing between my legs and using the wetness there as evidence that he was right. At the time, I thought he was. I grimace, trying to shake his words and the damage they did away.

Shane looks back up at me through his thick glasses, concern in his eyes as he misinterprets my reaction. "Y-yeah. I mean, it's not a deal-breaker. I just...I've always imagined having kids. Sorry, that's super weird to bring up on a first date—"

"I want kids, too," I interrupt, placing my hand on top of his. He startles and flushes at my touch, and a long moment passes between us. It feels like he can see into my soul and I'm seeing my dreams reflected in his eyes.

"You'd be a great mom, I bet."

"Hah! You're the first person to say that. Is it the age difference? Because if you want to call me mommy, you can."

His face turns scarlet, and he chokes on his drink. "N-no! I'm not...is it hot in here?"

I squeeze his hand, then let it go and sit back to take in the sight of him so flustered. A vision of domestic life with Shane as a co-parent flashes through my eyes, like some kind of portent. Him pulling a batch of muffins out of the oven and fending off the vulture-like circling of our three girls, while I help our youngest with his math homework at a cluttered dining table. It feels so real.

I worry that I've stopped breathing as waves of overwhelming happiness and love from my fantasy family wash over me.

Shaking the vision away, I grin at him like a fool. "I think you'd be an amazing dad. I can totally see you hauling a pack of kids to dance classes and making brownies for a bake sale."

His expression relaxes, though I don't miss him adjusting his legs to hide his crotch. "I do bake a mean brownie, but birthday cakes are really where I shine."

"Damn, now I wish my birthday wasn't half a year away."

"Guess you'll just have to keep me around until then."

"I think I might keep you around a lot longer than that, witch." The words are out of my mouth before I can consider playing coy or taking things slow. But I don't care. I like Shane. A *lot*.

"I'd like that..." Shane clears his throat and runs a hand through his hair. "Do you want anything else? More coffee? Another pastry?"

I lick my lips. "I'm hungry for something else right now."

"I guess it is getting close to lunch. I think there's a pub around here that serves really good burgers. Unless you're sick of me."

Gods, he's too cute. "I was thinking of something else." I slide my chair back far enough that he gets a perfect view when I uncross my legs, flashing a hint of my bare pussy before crossing them again. He inhales sharply and a spike of his arousal hits me, making me shiver. "Come back to my place and I'll show you."

11

E lle holds my hand the entire walk back to her place, her thumb rubbing circles against my wrist heating my blood far more than it should. I've surreptitiously tucked my dick up into my waistband in a meager attempt to hide how embarrassingly hard I am thinking about what awaits me when we get to her townhouse. I can barely focus as she cheerfully chats about the weather, her neighbor's ancient dog she thinks is secretly a lich, and how she wants to train the pigeons on her roof to carry messages.

Wait, what? "Carrier pigeons?"

She laughs and squeezes my hand. "Was wondering if I'd lost you. You seem distracted."

"Maybe a little." I let out a feeble attempt at a laugh. "So, uh, pigeons, huh? I met a fae once that used ravens to watch the perimeter of his home for intruders. I could reach out and see if he has any advice."

She nods. "Oh, really? Security pigeons could be useful, but I'd really like to use them for correspondence."

"Hmm, I'm sure that the basic magic of communicating with the birds and coming to some sort of arrangement with them is the same..." Elle giggles, breaking me out of my thoughts about how to set up that kind of magic. "And you're messing with me."

She bats her eyelashes in an unconvincing display of innocence. "Me? Messing with you?" I mock frown at her and she laughs harder. Stepping in closer, she presses her hands onto my chest and licks her lips. "Alright, yes. But you're so fun to tease, Shane."

Shit, I'm hard as a rock again. So much for pigeon talk distracting me.

She laughs and tugs me along the short distance to her front steps, then releases my hand to unlock the door. I desperately try to get some control over my racing heart and the thrum of desire coursing through me—that spell was totally worthless. I'm on the edge already and she hasn't gotten anywhere near my dick.

"You coming?" she asks, holding the door open for me.

"Y-yeah." Gods, I hope she doesn't realize the double meaning of that for me right now.

The second I'm through the door, Elle grabs my shoulders and shoves me against the wall, her purse clattering to the floor. She presses in, caging me in place despite her shorter frame. "I'm so hungry, Shane. Are you going to let me taste you?"

"F-fuck, yes." The words are out of my mouth for less than a second before her lips crash against mine. She consumes me, her tongue slipping into my mouth in a needy kiss. I groan at her taste. A mixture of coffee, sweet pastries, and a unique, tingling heat. Returning the kiss with equal fervor, my hands move to her hips, fingers digging into the soft flesh there as I resist the urge to grind against her.

She nips at my lower lip, then pulls back, both of us panting from the intensity of that kiss. It felt life-altering. I'll never be the same after kissing Elle.

"Elle...That was..."

"Fuck, you taste even better than I thought you would." Her lips descend to my neck, pressing hot kisses and nips down the side that make my legs weak. "So good."

I'm vibrating with the need to kiss her again, but she drops to her knees, her hands trailing down my chest to rest against my thighs, framing my erection.

I let out an undignified, choked sound as she leans in and places a kiss against my clothed cock. She giggles as it jerks against her touch and looks up at me with a predatory gleam in her eyes. My balls draw up and my cock twitches again at the sight.

Fuck, don't come yet!

"Mmm, I bet this tastes even better. Do you want my mouth on your cock, Shane?"

"Y-you don't have to, I—"

Her other hand squeezes my thigh, her nails digging in enough to cause a prick of pain that makes me even harder. "That's not an answer. Do you want me to suck your cock until you come down my throat, witch?"

"Oh fuck." I gasp as she emphasizes her point with another press of her lips to my aching length through my pants. "Y-yes! I want that. Please."

"Good boy. Already begging so sweetly." Elle makes quick

work of my belt and zipper, her hand delving into my boxer briefs to pull out my cock rather than pushing my pants off. It throbs against her grip, the tip swollen red and leaking a long trail of pre-cum.

"It's been a long time since I've sucked a witch's cock." She gathers the moisture at the tip with her finger, bringing it to her lips and licking it off. The sight is nearly my undoing, and my nails dig into my palms to maintain control. "Is there magic in your cum? It tastes...sweet. I want more."

Her head dips down and her tongue swipes across the head of my cock, licking away a fresh bead of pre-cum. Where her tongue touched, there's the same tingling heat I felt when we kissed. It's incredible.

"Ah! No, I don't think so, but I've never..." My neck and face burn as I realize what I just said.

"You've never what?" Elle lazily slides her hand up and down my length in a light stroke. "Never tasted your cum?"

My face gets even hotter. "N-no, I..."

"Mmm, dirty boy. So you know how good you taste." She punctuates her words by licking a long stripe from the base of my cock to the tip.

"Oh, gods." My balls draw up even tighter and I feel like I'm moments away from coming and blasting my load over her face. Which is not the way I want to end our first date.

"So then, what have you never done?"

Fuck, I'm going to come. I take in a shuddering breath and decide to be honest, in case that might save my dignity. "No one's ever... done this."

Her brows shoot up, but she quickly schools her expression. "You're telling me that no one else has had the pleasure of tasting this perfect cock? Of sucking you dry?"

I nod, unable to get words out through the mixture of shame and arousal coursing through me.

"Their loss." She winks up at me before wrapping her lips around my cock and sucking it down to the base, her throat convulsing against me as her nails bite into my ass, holding me in place.

"Fuck!" I shout, feeling my release barreling toward me. "Fuck, oh god, I'm—" My vision narrows as she swallows against my cock and moans. I'm on the precipice, about to tumble over, excruciating tension buzzing through me.

But the release doesn't come.

Elle pulls off, sucking in a breath and giving me a questioning look, before taking me down her throat again. Her head bobs, tongue swirling against the head of my cock on each upstroke.

I'm shaking, tears welling in my eyes as the sensation just keeps building. "Elle, I—oh gods!"

"That's it. Give it to me. I want your cum," she moans as she pulls off for a moment, before sucking me with even more maddening motions, her hand moving to fondle my balls.

I feel lightheaded and the edges of my vision darken, my legs threatening to give out on me. "S-stop, I can't..." I moan, in pleasure-pain.

She immediately pulls back, her hands coming up to my hips to steady me. "What's wrong? Are you okay? Oh Shane, I'm so sorry! I didn't mean to go too fast."

"It's not...you didn't...I can't—"

"It's okay. You don't need to explain." She helps me down to sit on the floor, brushing my hair off of my face with a tenderness that makes my chest squeeze. When I look into her eyes, she looks ashamed.

Fuck.

I reach out to cup her face, pushing down another shudder as the need to orgasm pulses through me. "You d-didn't do anything wrong. I'm just a fucking idiot."

"Not being ready for sex isn't—"

"I used a sex spell!" I blurt out, cutting off her sweet, unnecessarily kind words.

"What?"

"I used a sex spell. After the night at the club, after I, uh, made a mess of myself, I didn't want to lose control again. So I found a spell and cast it last night, just in case I couldn't keep it together around you again. Looks like it works. I just didn't know that it'd keep me from coming entirely."

Elle blinks at me for a long, uncomfortable moment, before her lips twist into a devilish grin. "So you're telling me I can tease you for as long as I want and you won't be able to come?"

My cock jerks painfully, and I hiss. "Fuck. Yes. But..."

"Poor baby, look at you." She slides a fingertip down my cock, which weeps with pre-cum and jerks again at her touch. "So needy. Desperate for relief."

"Oh gods, I can't!"

Elle wraps her hand around my cock and I almost sob at how good and terrible it feels. But she tucks my aching length back into my pants, gently redoing the zipper and my belt before drawing back. "I won't torture you any more. At least not today."

"Thank you," I gasp, sucking in choked breaths as I try to come down from the edge.

Elle pats my leg and goes to grab me a glass of water. After what feels like an eternity, my cock finally goes down and I'm able to stand up from the floor.

She guides me to her couch, carefully sitting in the chair across from me as if she knows getting too close will turn me on again.

"I'm so sorry, Elle. Shit, I can't imagine what you must think of me."

"Don't apologize. Though, maybe don't do any sex spells without letting me know going forward. I only want to torture you if you want me to. Speaking of which, you need a safeword."

"A what?"

"A safeword. When you're begging me to stop but you actually want more, there needs to be a word other than 'stop' or 'no' that you can use."

My cock twitches at the idea. "Oh."

"Don't worry about it now. We can talk when you're not so...on edge."

"Thanks." I huff out a weak laugh. "Wait...you want to see me again?"

She smiles back at me and my heart leaps. "Yes. I think you mentioned something about getting dinner and discussing our deepest secrets. Though, I owe you one now since you've already told me about being inexperienced."

"Yeah, it's the least you can do after I told you I'm a virgin." My self-deprecating chuckle peters out as her eyes widen. "Shit. I guess I could have had sex and never had a blow job. Way to play it cool, Shane."

"Virginity is an outdated human construct. I don't care if you've fucked a thousand or zero people. I can't get any diseases, and I can tell you have some kind of warding magic on you for that and contraception. Do you care how many people I've fucked?"

"I—I..." There is a small, self-hating part of me that cares because I worry I'll never measure up to her other partners. But should I tell her that? Fuck it, hiding things has only made a mess of things so far. "I don't judge you or think anything bad about you for how many partners you've had. It's just hard for me to believe that I'll be able to compare to them."

"If how hard you made me come the other night from just your fingers is any indication, you'll do fine. Plus, part of the fun of sex is figuring out how to get your partner off and bring each other the most pleasure. You'll be a fast learner, especially with an experienced teacher like me." I flush at her praise. "I like you, Shane. This isn't just about getting off for me. And I'm pretty sure it's the same for you. So try to relax about the sex stuff. I promise I'm the last person who would judge you—whether you come in your pants or can't come at all." She winks at me to emphasize that last point.

"Thank you. I like you too, Elle. It's definitely not just about sex."

"Good. Now I should probably let you go home and ride out the rest of that spell."

I groan. "As much as I'd like to stay, you're right. I don't think I can stay calm around you." I gesture down to my semi-hard cock. "I'll call you to make dinner plans, if that's okay? Oh wait, you owe me a secret!"

"Hah! Hmm, let's see. Oh! No, not that one..."

"You can tell me anything. I promise I won't judge."

Elle fidgets with the hem of her dress, looking uncharacteristically nervous. "I've never had someone fall in love with me. Lust, sure. There were a few times I thought maybe, but it wasn't...they weren't. Sometimes I worry there's something wrong with me." She laughs, but the amusement doesn't reach her eyes.

I stare back, unable to formulate a reply for a moment. This lovely, charming woman thinks she's unlovable? It's absurd. "They were fools if they couldn't recognize how lovable you are."

Her expression softens, her eyes growing molten at my words. "I want to kiss you. Can you handle that in your current state?"

I'm off the couch and pulling her up into a kiss before I can worry about getting too turned on. I don't care. It's worth it to feel her lips on mine. As I hold her, my stomach flutters in a way that has nothing to do with how much I need to come.

She feels perfect. Like she was sent from the gods, despite her demonic heritage. I...I'm not in love with her yet. That would be crazy. But I can imagine loving her. I can imagine kissing her like this every day for the rest of my life.

12

ELLE

"So how've you been? You're looking especially good tonight. Happier than I've seen in a while." The handsome mothman sitting across from me gestures to the grin that's been on my face for the last week.

My smile grows even wider and if my skin wasn't already pink, I'm sure I'd appear flushed. "I'm good. Really good. How are you, Rowan?"

His mottled brown wings flutter and spread out a bit as he leans forward to grab his whiskey. "Oh, you know...the usual. Busy and stressed, but okay. Job's fine. Tomas is still an angel, thank the gods."

Rowan is a regular at Heaven's Door, though he doesn't come in nearly as often since he took custody of his sister's baby. We've bonded over time, and now when he visits, it's like seeing an old friend rather than a patron. He always gets a private room, but just wants to chat and hang out in our monster forms.

"Well, I'm glad you could make it out to see me! It's been a while, hasn't it?"

"Too long!" He sighs as he takes another sip of his drink, the tightness in his shoulders easing.

"You need some help with that tension?" I wink at him, knowing he's not likely to take me up on the offer of a lap dance.

"Tempting, but I think I'll stick with talking tonight. Unless you need to feed?"

"I'll be fine. I...I'm seeing someone, so my hunger is more focused these days."

"Oh, that's exciting. Please tell me it isn't that asshole from before." Rowan grimaces as he thinks about my terrible ex.

"No! He's a witch and a total sweetheart. I really like him."

Rowan cocks an eyebrow. "Why am I sensing a but?"

"He's perfect! I want him so much. And not just for sex. But gods, I want that too."

I've been in a constant state of hunger since Shane and I started dating, and feeding from patrons at the club doesn't fully sate it. I crave *him*. We've been on dates almost every day over the past week, but I haven't made another move since that morning after coffee. The more time we spend together, the more certain I am in my affection for him. I don't want to scare him off or push him away.

"Wait." His eyes widen. "You're not sleeping with him?"

"Ugh, I really shouldn't be telling you this. Promise me this stays in this room, Ro."

He nods solemnly. "I promise. Is it something terrible? Did a hag curse his dick off or something?"

I laugh at the thought, some of my worry easing. "He's a virgin. Which wouldn't be a problem, but he's so worried about performing and coming too soon. I don't want to pressure him to go too fast or make him uncomfortable. So I'm waiting for him to make the next move."

"Wow, I can see why that'd be tricky. Poor guy, he must be jacking off 24/7 if he's dating you and you're not fucking."

"He's not the only one! I've gone through an entire pack of batteries from how much I've used my vibrators."

Rowan gives me a sympathetic frown. "Oof yeah, it must be a special kind of torture for you to feel how hot you make him, but not do anything about it. May I make a suggestion? As a guy who also worried about losing his virginity."

"Please. I feel completely lost."

"I know you're worried about pushing him, but he might need your help to take that step. Right now, he's probably psyching himself out. You're a succubus, after all. A literal demon of lust." He gestures to my horns.

Shane *is* definitely the type to overthink and worry about things. "I'm not sure how to help him without being too aggressive."

Rowan chuckles and shrugs. "Take the focus off of him. Make it about you and your pleasure. I know you get off on other people's arousal, but surely you wouldn't object to a few regular orgasms from a guy eager to please."

Heat pools in my low belly. "No, I wouldn't." I'd feel silly for not seeing the obvious solution, but I'm usually so focused on the desires of my partners that it didn't even cross my mind.

"There! Problem solved." Rowan dusts off his hands. "Now, I

think I will take you up on that dance because it seems like you could really use it."

I grin back at him and stand, sensing his arousal seeping into the air as I move closer. "How very generous of you. I know how torturous it is to stare at my tits and have me grind on your cock."

"A burden I'm willing to bear for my dear friend." He licks his lips, hands coming to my shoulders as I move onto his lap. "Wait. Will your boyfriend be pissed if you do this?"

My heart flutters at the use of the word "boyfriend". Shane and I haven't defined our budding romance yet. Though I know he doesn't exude any jealousy when I mention work and the club. "Nope. He knows I enjoy my work."

"Huh. He sounds like a good guy."

I roll my hips, closing my eyes for a second as Shane's handsome face fills my mind. "He's the best."

IT'S BEEN the best week of my life. Elle and I have gone on four daytime dates to accommodate her shifts at the club and my surprising influx of new clients.

After I reached out to the paranormal council about the coven's unethical summoning, the next day I had three messages with job requests. I'd thought that narcing on the sex coven would hurt me, but apparently the monsters in this city respect integrity in their private investigators.

Every time I see Elle, I grow more enamored with her. She's so much more than meets the eye—clever and knowledgeable, with a tender and generous heart. Shockingly, she seems to find just as much merit in me. Though I know she's struggling with my timidity when it comes to sex.

It's also been the hardest week of my life—double entendre very much intended. It's not that I don't want to sleep with her. Gods, that's all I can think about half the time. I just...I'm scared. She told me she won't judge me, but what if I'm awful? What if I come right away again or can't stay hard? What if I flop on top of her like a beached whale or don't have enough stamina and turn into a sweaty, wheezing mess? I've tried doing some research, but don't trust any of the spells in my books since that disaster where it took a day for me to stop having an erection.

I need to get my shit together soon, because we have our first dinner date tonight. I made a bold claim about tasting her pussy—still don't know where that came from. Just the thought makes my cock swell. To have her laid out for me, ready for me to touch and taste as she moans my name. At least, I hope that's what happens. More likely I'll be so incompetent that she'll tell me to stop after a few minutes.

My phone rings, startling me from my anxious thoughts. I race over to grab it in case it's Elle, but Nathan's gravelly voice greets me instead.

"Hey dude! How's it going?"

He sounds cheerful, which means one of two things—he's found a new girlfriend or he needs a favor. "Hey! Things are good. How are you?"

"Great! Are you busy right now? I found this guy who's selling a brand new white leather sofa for half price. It would be amazing in my place. You know how barren it looks since Vanessa took half the furniture."

Ah, so it's a favor. Damn. Not that I don't want to help him, but he could really use something to distract him from his ex. "Oh nice! You need any help moving it?"

"Could you? I'd owe you big time. We could grab some beers, make an event of it!"

"I'm happy to help. I have to say no to the drinks though. I, uh, I have a date tonight."

"Oh shit! So things turned out well with that girl you were calling, I take it?"

"Yeah. Really well."

Nathan laughs. "Damn, you're in love! I can hear it in your voice."

"N-no! I mean, I really like her. She's amazing. But it's too soon for that."

"Sure, sure. Just remember this conversation when I'm making a toast at your wedding."

I immediately picture Elle in a lacy white gown that hugs her curves, wings trailing behind her as she walks down the aisle with a bouquet of pink roses that match her skin. Shit, stop thinking about what she'd look like in a wedding gown! I don't even know if she'd want that kind of wedding. "Hah, yeah, okay. Give me a few and I'll head over to your place."

"WHEN YOU SAID you needed to move a couch, I didn't think you meant an enormous sectional," I grumble as we make the last push to hoist the white leather behemoth up the stairs of Nathan's apartment building. By the time we get it into his place, I'm out of breath and drenched in sweat.

Nathan just laughs, lifting the hem of his t-shirt to wipe the sweat off his face, showing off a ridiculous set of abs. He doesn't seem tired at all. I should ask him about his workout routine. Shit, I hope Elle doesn't expect me to have abs like that.

"Earth to Shane!" Nathan waves a hand in front of my face, knocking me out of my spiraling thoughts. "You okay, dude?"

My overheated brain must lack the normal filter that I have, because I blurt out the first thing that comes to mind. "I don't know how to eat pussy!"

His eyes grow comically large. "Uh, what?"

"It's hopeless! Elle is a sex goddess and I'm a nerdy virgin loser who's never even gone down on a woman before."

"Ah. Right."

"You agree! I should just cancel our date and let her go out with someone who knows what the hell they're doing."

Nathan shakes his head. "Whoa, man. Chill out. That's not the answer! And I don't think you're hopeless. You just don't have any experience. Does she know that?"

"She does. She says it's okay, but she's a succubus! Of course it's not okay."

"Holy shit, you're dating a *succubus*? Why didn't you lead with that?"

"Not helping!" I scrub my face with my hand, letting out a groan.

"Shit, sorry. That doesn't make a difference. I was just surprised." Nathan places his hands on my shoulders and locks eyes with me. "*You. Can. Do. This*. Take a deep breath."

I'm too hot and worried to care that I'm having a meltdown in front of Nathan, so I nod and do as he says.

"Again."

I take another deep breath, the tightness in my chest easing slightly.

"Good. Now, how much time do you have before your date?"

I glance down at my watch and frown. "Two hours."

"Perfect. Enough time for a pussy eating crash course."

"W-what?"

"Why do you think Vanessa stayed with me for as long as she did? It isn't because of my charming personality. Now sit down, keep breathing, and listen."

13

Nathan's lesson on eating pussy is one of the most humiliating thirty minutes of my life, but by the end, I'm not as freaked out about my date. By the time I get back to my place, shower, and change, there's no extra time to spend worrying, so I'm thankful for the couch moving as a distraction. Though I know my back won't agree with me in the morning.

Elle and I decided to meet at the restaurant, a small Italian place with intimate vibes. Neither of us have been before, but I've walked past it countless times, looking in at the dark red booths and low-lighting, wondering what it would be like to have someone to go there with. Now I'm not only eating there, but I'm going with the most incredible person I've met.

A chilly breeze rustles through the trees lining the sidewalk, signaling that our unusually temperate autumn has ended. It feels good on my face, cooling off some of the anxious heat that's still simmering inside me. When I arrive at the restaurant, Elle's already waiting outside. My heart speeds up as she waves, approaching with a brilliant smile on her face. I still can't understand why I'm able to elicit such a reaction from her.

I beam back at her, unable to suppress the mixture of excitement, affection, and arousal I feel in her presence. "Hey! Sorry I'm la—"

She cuts me off, closing the rest of the distance and bringing her mouth to mine in a kiss that makes my breath shudder out in a sigh. When our lips part, I grin at her like a fool. "Hey..."

"Hello Shane." Gods, the way she says my name makes my cock twitch. She says it like it's an intimate secret between us. Elle steps back and gives me a once over. "You look very handsome tonight."

"Th-thanks." My cheeks warm despite the cold air outside. "You look..." I pause, taking her in. She's wearing a bomber jacket over a skin-tight black dress, fishnets showing a tantalizing glimpse of her legs. With her heels, we're almost the same height, which oddly makes me more excited. She's so commanding and sexy that it's hard for me to tear my eyes away. "You look incredible."

"Thanks!" She kisses my cheek, giving me another chance to take in the soft scent of her perfume and the warm heat that is pure Elle. "Let's go inside. I'm starving."

By the way she looks at me, I can tell food's not the only thing she's hungry for. Gods, help me be enough for her tonight.

MANEATER

Dinner goes by in a blur. One moment, we're getting seated in a cozy corner booth and the next, my plate of spaghetti carbonara is clean. Elle sighs contentedly and leans back after the waiter clears our plates. "Mmm, that was excellent. Thank you again for dinner."

"Of course! Um..." My eyes dart down to the dessert menu. I pick it up, trying to hide the slight shaking of my hand as I get ready to set us down the path I planned for tonight. "Would you like some dessert? It looks like they have tiramisu."

Elle perks up, leaning forward with a lazy grin. "That's my favorite."

I know. That was one of the first things I asked about on our coffee date. "Yeah." I swallow heavily, hoping she can't tell how nervous I am for what I'm implying by getting this dessert. My words from our encounter at the strip club echo in my mind. *I want to go to dinner and discuss our deepest secrets, then order your favorite dessert. I want to taste it on your tongue and then take you home and see if it's anywhere as sweet as your pussy.*

"Dessert sounds wonderful. I think I saved enough room." She winks at me and laughs softly when I flush.

After the waiter stops by and we order dessert, silent tension builds between us. Elle seems to love it, watching me across the table with a gleam in her eyes. Part of me loves it too, but my nerves force me to fill the conversational lull.

"I got so caught up in our conversation, I totally forgot to ask about your secrets. Apologies for falling short of my promise from the other night."

"Ooh, yes. Why don't you go first?"

"Alright...how deep do we want to go?"

"I want you to go really deep, Shane." Elle licks her lips and leans even further forward, the neckline of her dress dipping down to show off her cleavage.

I let out a very undignified laugh-snort. "I walked into that one, didn't I?"

She giggles and nods. "You catch on quick. Now tell me your secrets."

The way she's looking at me, I would tell her everything. Do anything she asks of me. "Okay..." I go with the first thing I can think of. It isn't a secret as much as something that hasn't come up yet. Something that I'm hoping isn't a problem, but if it is, then it'd be better to find out now. "I'm, uh...I'm not just attracted to women."

She waves a hand at me dismissively and smiles. "Neither am I."

"Oh! Well...good. So, that's not a problem for you?"

"No. It shouldn't be a problem for anyone, Shane." She sighs and reaches out to take my hand. "I'm sorry if anyone made you feel otherwise. People are bigoted jerks—fuck them and what they think." She softens her voice and squeezes my hand. "Thank you for telling me."

My eyes fill and I fight back the urge to cry at how simple that conversation was. "Gods, you're the best."

She grins at me. "I know!"

I laugh at her cheerful acceptance of her awesomeness, only releasing her hand when the waiter brings our desserts. The tiramisu is just as good as the rest of the food here, and I swear Elle plays up her moans and sighs of pleasure as she eats, licking her fork thoroughly with each bite.

"I know my secret wasn't very exciting, but what's yours?"

"Hmm...I'm an open book. No use in hiding things. Oh! There is one thing..."

I perk up, intrigued by what it could be. It's true that she's been very forthcoming so far. Something that makes me admire her even more.

"Okay so, promise me you won't judge me?"

I nod. "Of course. I would never."

"I wet myself when I was giving someone a lap dance."

My brows shoot up. "Do you mean that as a euphemism or—"

"No, I mean I pissed myself."

"Elle! Why?"

"You promised you wouldn't judge!" She scowls and throws her napkin at me.

"Sorry! Just...how much pee are we talking?"

"Not a full release situation, but more than a small leak. Enough that the guy noticed. I told him I'd squirted, but I don't think he bought it."

Tears prick my eyes as I laugh. "I have no room to judge given what happened to me when you...but *wow*."

She's laughing now too. "It's not like I did it on purpose! It was a really busy night, and I didn't realize how bad I needed to go until we were in the middle of things and he accidentally tickled me and well...now you know."

I wipe the tears from my eyes and grin back at her. "Thank you for sharing your shame with me. It makes me like you even more—which I didn't know was possible."

"I'm glad. I like you more now, too." Her eyes dip down in a rare moment of shyness. "I...I like you so much, Shane."

We lean forward until our mouths meet across the table in a slow kiss that stokes my desire for her even more. I taste the sweetness of the tiramisu on her tongue, but that's not what makes me lick my lips after we part.

Suddenly, I'm not so scared about what comes next tonight.

My chest squeezes, knowing this amazing woman cares for me. It's time for me to show her how much she means to me with more than words. "Do you want to come back to my place?"

Elle does a good job of masking her surprise, but I can tell she wasn't expecting me to ask that. She waves at the waiter to bring the check. "Gods, yes."

14

Something's shifted in Shane tonight. Nerves still simmer under the surface of his desire for me, but they're not as strong as before. When we get back to his apartment, he has a determined look in his eyes as he takes my hand and leads me inside.

His place is *amazing*. The apartment building and layout are nothing noteworthy, but bookshelves line the walls of the living area and hallway, giving the impression that he lives in a library. There's a comfy-looking dark brown couch across from a small brick fireplace, and on the mantle there's a small altar with crystals and candles for his spellwork. It should feel cluttered and claustrophobic with the sheer amount of books, but everything is neatly put in its place.

Everywhere I look, I find additional details that give me a glimpse into Shane's inner life. What I find tells a story of an intelligent, fascinating man.

When I finish my scan of his place, noting the tidy kitchen and the dining table that doubles as a workspace, I turn back to find him shifting in place, a sheepish smile on his face. "I know it's a lot of books. I'm a bit of a collector."

"I love it."

"Oh. Good!" He beams back at me like I just told him I loved him.

My cheeks heat at the thought. *You don't love him, Elle. That's silly. You're just infatuated and horny.* Speaking of which...

"So, did you bring me back here to admire your collection? Or did you want to give me a tour of the rest of the place?"

Shane's cheeks flush, but he nods. "R-right. Yes. We could go see my bedroom...just give me a minute!" He scurries away through a door on the other side of the living area, sending me an apologetic glance over his shoulder before quickly closing the door behind him.

Hmm, does he need a moment to psych himself up? Or maybe he left a mess of laundry in there that he wants to shove away in a closet. I smile to myself and inspect one of his bookshelves. My eyes are drawn to a collection of worn spellbooks, many in languages I can't read. I wonder if one of them has the sex magic spell he used the other day. I move to another shelf and my smile grows when I see a selection of romance novels. I'm reading the back blurb for *The Sea King's Captive,* when I hear the door open behind me.

"Interesting selection you have." I hold up the book, showing

Shane the scantily clad woman wrapped up in the tentacles of a crowned kraken.

Bright red splotches form on Shane's cheeks and neck. "That's—my grandma wrote romance novels, and she got me hooked on them. Not the ones she wrote! Just romance in general."

"Oh, how fun! Mind if I borrow this one?"

"Of course not!" Shane shifts in place, his eyes bouncing from my face to the floor, unable to hold my gaze for long. "Uh, would you like to see my bedroom?"

I set the book down and move closer, taking his hand in mine. "Yes. I'd love to."

"I...it's not as nice as yours, but..."

Shane leads me into his bedroom and warmth fills me as soon as I see what he's done. "Shane..."

Small motes of floating light hover near the ceiling like fireflies. Rose petals are strewn across the bed and a subtle scent of jasmine and vanilla fills the air. It's the most romantic thing anyone's ever done for me. Unexpected tears prick at my eyes. "This is wonderful. *You* are wonderful."

Shane's breath hitches at my words, and he squeezes my hand before pulling me against him. We hold each other for a long moment, gazing into each other's eyes. All I want to do is tear his clothes off and show him how wonderful I think he is, but I want to give him space to go at his own pace. So instead, I pull him down into a slow, lingering kiss.

As our tongues twine together, he deepens the kiss, hands sliding down to hold my hips and press our bodies even closer together. I let out a soft moan when I feel his hard length against my belly. Fuck, I need him so badly.

When our mouths part, Shane's pupils are blown wide and his

arousal calls out to me so powerfully it makes my knees weak. "I want to...may I taste you?"

Yes, gods, *finally*. My desire spikes, and I nod. "Yes. I need your mouth on me." I pull him with me until I'm sitting on the bed, my legs spreading so that he's standing between them. When I tug my skirt up and spread my legs further to show him the garter belt holding up my fishnets and my lack of panties, he groans.

"Fuck, Elle. You're so beautiful." He sinks to his knees, hands shaking slightly as he places them on my legs, then kisses the inside of my thigh. "I've wanted to do this since the night you let me touch you at the club. All I can think about in bed at night is how you sounded when you came."

I run a hand through his hair, looking down at him as he works his way up my thighs, kissing and caressing each inch of my flesh in a maddeningly slow ascent. He pauses for a moment to take off his glasses and set them in his shirt pocket with a shy smile. My other hand drops between my thighs to spread my pussy. "You wanted this? You wanted to lick my pussy and make me come on your face?"

"Y-yes. Please. I want to make you come, Elle. I...if I do something wrong..."

My hand slides down to caress his cheek, then lower to thumb his lip. "Don't worry, sweet witch. I'll tell you when I like something or when I want you to do something else. A good indicator is that I'll scream your name when I'm close." I fist my hand in his hair, pushing his face down to where I need him.

He moans and a moment later, his tongue is licking a stripe across my pussy that makes me gasp. He does it again and again, taking his time to explore all of me, dipping inside me for a moment, before sliding up to circle and tease my clit. It feels so fucking good. I can't believe he hasn't done this before.

Shane pulls away for a moment, and I have to suppress a whine. "Is that okay?"

"Yes! Now don't stop unless I tell you to!"

He smiles up at me from between my thighs, the affection and need in his gaze making my chest ache with an impossible feeling. It can't be love this soon, can it?

"Sorry!" His mouth is on me again, this time more confident in the movements of his tongue. He eats me out like I'm meant to be savored and he can't get enough of my taste. When he moans against me, I glance down to see his hand rubbing against the front of his pants.

"Take out your cock and stroke it while you eat my pussy. But don't come until I tell you to."

"F-fuck. I don't know if I can—"

I tighten my grip on his hair. "You can. Now stop talking and make me come."

His eyes widen for a moment before he's licking me again, his tongue swirling around my clit in steady motions that quickly build me toward my orgasm.

"Fuck, yes. That feels so good. You're doing so good."

He moans again and his fist on his cock pauses as he tries not to come. Our desire builds together, until I'm riding the intoxicating wave of it, ready for it to break at any moment.

"Oh gods, that's it. You're going to make me come. Come with me. *Now*."

It only takes one more swipe of his perfect tongue before my release hits me, holding his mouth to my pussy as I come harder than I have in years. As it crashes over me, his arousal surges right behind mine and it pushes me over the edge again. He groans against me, but doesn't stop licking me until I pull his mouth away and bring my lips down to meet his in a crushing kiss.

I'm gasping when we part, and Shane looks utterly wrecked kneeling before me. "Fuck. Shane. That was so good. Such a good boy."

He kisses my inner thigh, and I gasp when he nuzzles against my pussy. His eyes shine with need as he looks up at me. "Please let me make you come again."

Fuck me. There's no use in denying it now. This fluttering in my chest when I look at the man begging to make me come again feels a lot less like lust and much more like love.

15

I'm addicted to Elle's pussy. It's all I can think about since the other night when she let me make her come with my mouth three times. I love the heady taste, the way she soaked my face with her release, and the shuddering gasps she made when she came.

In retrospect, I wasn't giving myself enough credit when worrying about doing a good job. My magic helps me attune my perception to minute changes around me. After a few times of hearing her breath catch, feeling her clit throb under my tongue, and sensing the thickening of her arousal in the air, I learned what gives her the most pleasure. Grinding her cunt against my face as I fucked my tongue inside her, sucking her clit right when she's almost at her peak, and my own moans of pleasure seem to work best. Shit, just thinking about how she cried my name the last time I made her come is making me hard.

Who am I kidding? I'm addicted to Elle, period. I soak up her warm presence like the sun every time we're together. Which has been almost every day for the past two weeks. Samhain's only three days away, and I should figure out my plans for any spell-work I want to do while the veil is thin. Instead, I spend my spare time thinking about how I can make Elle smile the next time we're together. And gathering up the courage to fuck her with more than my tongue.

I've learned to control my cock a bit more, but she's still so overwhelming. I'd be happy to keep eating her pussy while I fist my dick, but I know she wants more. At night, sometimes I imagine more, too. Visions of Elle shifting into her true form and riding my face as she fucks me with her tail. But surely she wouldn't want to do that. Fucking me like that is probably too far, even for her. That doesn't keep me from imagining how amazing it would feel for her to have complete control over me. I even add restraints into the fantasy sometimes—me tied to the bed as she takes what she needs from my body.

Gods, I wish I could see her today. But I needed to catch up on some surveillance and PI contracts that I've put off, and she has a shift tonight. I almost forgot that tonight is game night, but thank-fully Stacy called to offer help setting up since we'd planned to have some snacks and spooky decorations to celebrate Halloween. When I'm done with work for the day, I scramble to bake the fingerbone breadsticks and graveyard cake, forgoing the ghost cookies for the sake of time.

By the time Mark and Nathan arrive, we've transformed my apartment into a spooky lair thanks to Stacy's fae skills and my illusion magic. I'm glad all my D&D friends are monsters, because explaining the illusory bats flapping around my entry hall to non-paranormals would be tough.

When I emerge from my bedroom after quickly getting changed into my slightly lame vampire costume, Nathan and Stacy are already digging into the snacks, while Mark's eyes rove over Stacy in her Princess Leia costume as she's turned away. Damn, she's really tormenting him tonight with that—he went to see Return of the Jedi three times earlier this year.

"Dude! Nice costume." Nathan grins as I flash my fake fangs. "The whole Dracula vibe suits your pale ass."

I snort and roll my eyes at him. "Thanks. What are you supposed to be?"

He adjusts his black cat ears and gestures down at his black-and-white striped shirt. "A cat burglar. Duh."

I snort at the dumb joke. "Hah, right. Mark, that's a really impressive costume!"

Mark tears his eyes away from where they're glued on Stacy's ass and looks down at his handmade, incredibly detailed Star Trek uniform, complete with phaser. "Oh, thanks!"

Once everyone's grabbed their snacks and drinks, we settle in around my dining table. "Alright, are you ready to face your doom?" Mark meets my cheerful grin with a groan, no doubt still pissed about Stacy rushing in last session, while the others give an excited cheer.

WHEN I PULL into the parking lot at Heaven's Door, the outside lights aren't on yet. The sun is just setting, so I'm not worried about my safety, but I'll have to let someone know when I get inside. As I approach the employee entrance, I see there's a note pasted on the door.

> Closed tonight—generator busted. Sorry to anyone I couldn't get a hold of before they headed in for work!
> —Ariel.

Well, shit. My boss must have called, and I missed the message. I turn to see Tiffany getting out of her car and wave. At least I'm not the only one who drove out here tonight.

"Hey Elle! What's up?"

"Looks like the power's out. Ari left a note on the door saying we're closed tonight."

Tiffany groans. "Damn. Think I can get the boss to reimburse me for driving my ass over here for no reason?"

I shake my head with a smile. "If you ask her, you're braver than I am. She said she tried to call, but I missed her message."

"Hah. Probably best to just let it go and take advantage of the night off for a change. See you tomorrow if the power's back? Unless you wanna go grab a drink or something."

Tiffany is fun, but when presented with a rare night off, my mind goes to Shane. "Thanks, but I think I'll go surprise my boyfriend."

"Whoa, boyfriend?! Girl, you have got to tell me more. Wait, is it that nerdy guy that came to see you?"

"Yep!" I say proudly, daring her to make a comment about how he's not my usual type.

"Thank God. Sorry, it's just that Drea said she talked to him and he was super sweet and nothing like the, uh—fuck it, nothing like the assholes you've dated before. I know I shouldn't say that, but they *sucked*, Elle."

A laugh bursts from my chest at her disgusted expression. "They did, didn't they?"

"But this one's different?" She gives me a knowing look.

"Yeah. So different. I think...I think he might be *the one*."

Tiffany's eye go wide. "No shit? Well, then get the hell out of here and go see your man. Just don't forget to invite me to the wedding!"

I giggle and nod. "I will!" My mind flashes to images of a traditional succubus binding ceremony. Shane tied up like an offering as he recites the infernal oaths of dedication to me. And then the subsequent consummation in front of all our ceremony's guests. I'm not sure he'd be into that part, so maybe we can make it a hybrid ceremony. I've always looked good in white.

It's too soon to think about marrying him. It's too soon. It's too—ah, screw it. It's not like I'm proposing to him tonight. What does it hurt for me to daydream a bit?

Thoughts of a combination succubus binding and traditional church wedding swirl through my head on the short drive to Shane's building. I have to force them away as I climb the stairs to his apartment, my heart racing with excitement about seeing him.

I knock on his door, taking a second to fluff up my hair and adjust my tits in my bra so there's more cleavage showing. Long moments pass and a sick sense of dread fills me.

What if he doesn't want to see me?

What if he's in there with someone else?

Bad memories flash through my head—exes caught cheating and acting like it was no big deal because I'm a succubus, and people I loved acting put out by my presence once the thrill of sex with me lost its novelty. I know logically that Shane isn't like them, but the panic has already set in.

Fuck, I should go. This was a mistake.

Before I can make my escape, the door opens and Shane appears. In a...vampire costume?

"Elle! Hey, what are you—" He scans my face and his surprised smile falls when he notices the tears welling in my eyes. "Shit, what's wrong? Are you okay? Are you hurt?!"

I shake my head, but traitorous tears slide down my cheeks. "I-I'm okay"

His arms wrap around me, pulling me into a tight hug. "Shh, it's okay. What's going on?"

I cling to him, hiding my face against his chest as I try to compose myself. "I-I just wanted to see you."

He presses a kiss to my hair and rubs my back in soothing circles. When I pull back to wipe my tears away and look up at him, his lip quirks in a playful way that makes my chest squeeze. "You're upset you wanted to see me?"

I let out a weak laugh. "No! There was a power outage at the club, so I thought I'd come surprise you. But then when I got here, it brought up some unpleasant memories. It's nothing you did. I'm always so happy to see you. I just...sometimes I worry that you'll stop feeling the same way."

"Oh, Elle. I understand why that would upset you. Though, if I stop wanting to see you, please call a doctor because something has gone horribly wrong with my brain." He dips his head down to kiss me, but stops and gives me a sheepish smile. "Almost forgot about the fangs."

My brow raises at the sight of the plastic fangs in his mouth. "*Did* I interrupt something? Or do you just dress as Dracula in your spare time?"

Shane laughs. "It's my gaming group. We're having a little Halloween celebration tonight, but I can ask them to leave—"

"Hey! Who's out there?" a deep voice calls from inside his apartment.

Shane glares back toward his apartment. "Hold on!"

"Oh! That sounds like fun. Call me when you're done, if it's not too late?" I lean in to kiss his cheek, but when I move to back away, he holds me in place.

"Stay. I'm sure my friends would love to meet you and it'll be a good distraction from the bloodbath happening in the game. I mean, only if you want to! But if you do, please stay."

"Shane, come on!" the deep voice sounds closer and a moment later a muscular man wearing cat ears appears behind Shane in the doorway. "Oh shit, is this Elle?" His bright smile gleams against his dark brown skin. *"Holy fuck, dude,"* he adds in a stage whisper.

Shane turns pink and gives me an apologetic look, but his friend is already reaching out a hand to me. "Nice to meet you! I'm Nathan, Shane's best friend. I've heard so much about you."

I take his hand and give it a shake, smiling back. "Good things, I hope."

"Of course! My man here is totally smitten." Shane turns an even darker shade of pink. "You joining us? Please say yes! I need someone to help me diffuse the sexual tension between the crushing doofuses in there."

"Ooh, that sounds fun. Though you might be asking the wrong person to help you there."

"Right, because of being a succubus. Hah! In that case, maybe you'll help push them over the edge. Because if I have to sit through one more D&D session with them bickering and eye-fucking each other, I'm going to scream."

I laugh as Shane shakes his head at his friend's rant. "Now I'm even more intrigued. You sure you don't mind me crashing your party?

Shane and Nathan say "no" in unison, and Shane takes my hand in his. "I'm so glad you're here," he whispers, shooting me an adoring look.

"Me too. Now sit back and let me help get your friends to fuck."

16

SHANE

My palms sweat as I lead Elle into my apartment to meet my friends. She gasps at the decorations, delighting in the screeches of my bat illusions and Stacy's transformation of my bookshelves into dank cave walls. Nathan scurries ahead of us, no doubt to tell Stacy and Mark we have a guest.

"I feel like I should have a costume. This is so spooky and fun!" Elle leans in to kiss my cheek before we round the corner into the dining area.

"Hmm, I might have something in my closet." Her eyes light up. "Use whatever you want. Let me introduce you to the rest of the group first."

Mark and Stacy are over by the snacks, and Stacy almost drops her slice of cake when she sees Elle.

"Hi everyone! Sorry for crashing game night. I'm Elle, Shane's girlfriend." She beams at the pair with a beautiful smile, and my pulse races when she introduces herself as my *girlfriend*.

Mark recovers more quickly from the onslaught of Elle's charm, setting his plate down to come over and shake her hand. "Nice to meet you, Elle! I'm Mark."

"You're...I'm...*wow, Shane*." Stacy murmurs, then shakes her head like she's waking from a stupor. "Sorry! I've never seen someone so pretty before in my life. I'm Stacy. I'll stop acting so weird in a second, I promise."

"I never mind someone saying I'm pretty," Elle says with a giggle, and Stacy flushes. "You look amazing, Stacy! Love the costume. And Mark, that costume looks like it could be from a TV set. It's so good. Though I can't help thinking you'd make a perfect Han Solo."

Nathan shoots her a thumbs up from behind Mark and Stacy's backs, and I have to suppress a snort at her first step in bringing the two together.

"I'm going to see if I can cobble a costume together from Shane's closet real quick because it feels wrong to be here without one. Do you want to help me, Stacy?"

Stacy takes a few moments to get her reply out. "Y-yeah! Sure."

"Wonderful! Be back in a few minutes, boys. Don't get into too much trouble without us." Elle tugs me into a quick kiss, her tongue darting out to slide against my lips teasingly.

Gods, she's incredible. Less than five minutes with my friends and she's already charmed them all. Not that I had any doubt she would. I'm the one that's an awkward mess sometimes.

"So, Elle...Where did you two meet? Because, *damn*." Mark grins at me before popping a chip into his mouth.

"It's uh, a funny story...um..."

"Shane found a coven to join, but they were sex cultists and Elle was a succubus they summoned!" Nathan blurts out, then shoots me a sheepish look.

Gods, I should never have told him.

Mark cocks a brow at me. "Never took you for a sex cult kind of guy, Shane."

"I'm not. I didn't know that's what they were!"

"Sure, sure."

"I didn't! I helped break Elle out of the summoning circle once I realized what was going on and then, uh, we talked for a bit and she said she was interested in me. I thought at first it was just her being kind after I helped her, but it turns out she likes me. Gods know why."

Nathan frowns at me. "Come on, man. You're a catch. Smart, kind, funny, and pretty hot. For a pasty white dude, at least."

Mark nods in agreement, shocking me. "You're a good-looking guy, Shane. If I wasn't so into Sta—I mean, if I didn't want to mess up our friendship, I would've thought about asking you out."

"W-wait, really?" Mark's a handsome guy. Way out of what I thought my league would be. Plus, I didn't know he's bi.

"Yeah, yeah, you're a rad hottie. *Whatever*. What was that about being into Stacy?!" Nathan grins at Mark like he's prey caught in his trap.

"I didn't...I don't...fuck! Yes, I'm into Stacy. But if your wolfy ass says one damn thing about it, I will kill you."

"I won't say anything. But dude. She's *so* into you. It's obvious! Why aren't you doing anything about it?"

"She's not. I asked her out a few months ago, and she turned me down."

A few months ago... "That was when she was slammed at work. Are you sure it wasn't just bad timing?"

"Ugh, I don't know. But she said no, so I'm not going to ask her again. I don't want to be that creep who can't take a hint."

"Maybe you can let her know subtly that you're still interested. Like tell her she looks nice or compliment her when she does something cool in the game." Nathan takes a swig of his beer, then continues. "As things are right now, she probably thinks you hate her."

"I don't hate her! Shit." Mark fidgets with the badge on his costume. "Can we talk about something else?"

Nathan takes a bigger swig of his drink and grimaces. "Vanessa's dating a guy from my gym. A huge beefcake. Literally, since he's a minotaur."

"Shit, that blows." Mark places a sympathetic hand on Nathan's shoulder.

"Thanks, dude. I know I gotta move on, so this is the kick in the tail I needed. Just wish I were lucky enough to find someone amazing, like the two of you."

"You will," I say, adamantly.

"I don't know. Neither of you said I was hot," Nathan sighs.

Mark rolls his eyes. "You know you're hot. You don't need us to stroke your ego."

"What's that about stroking?" Elle's voice carries from the living room and I turn, almost choking on my soda when I see her "costume".

She's in her succubus form, a white sheet wrapped around her in a toga that dips low enough in the back to accommodate her wings and tail. The fabric is opaque enough to cover her body, but it clings to her, showing off every dip and curve. The whole thing is definitely being held up by magic, no doubt Stacy's doing.

Nathan whistles. "Damn! Elle, you're even prettier in this form. You sure you're set on Shane?"

I glare at Nathan, but Elle just laughs and moves to my side, threading her arm through mine. "I'm sure."

Stacy is even more flushed than she was before she went into my bedroom with Elle, and her eyes keep darting over to Mark. Elle must have said something to her.

"I—I meant to say this earlier...Stacy, you look incredible. You're so beau—uh, that costume looks great on your body—on you!" All eyes in the room shift over to Mark, who looks shocked by his own words.

Stacy stares back at Mark like he's grown a second head. Silence fills the room and for a moment I worry that Mark was right about Stacy not liking him. "Mark, can I talk to you in private for a minute?"

"Uh, sure..." Mark looks dumbfounded as he and Nathan exchange a quick glance. Now I really hope we weren't wrong about Stacy liking him. She heads back into my bedroom, Mark following behind her and shutting the door.

"Is she going to kill him?" Nathan asks, eyes wide.

"In a sense," Elle says, casually striding over to the snacks and filling a plate. "Oh wow, Shane, did you make this cake? It looks delicious!"

"In a sense?! What do you mean? Should I go in there?" Nathan's eyes dart over to my bedroom.

Elle shrugs. "Not unless you want to see them fucking. By the time our girl Stacy is done with that boy, he'll be seeing the gods."

I blink at her, processing her words. "Wait. What? They're in there having sex right now? In my room?"

"Yep! Don't worry, I'll buy you new sheets, love." Elle grins at me, and Nathan lets out a choked laugh.

"Holy shit, Elle! You're a goddess. How did you do it?"

"I honestly didn't have to do anything. The second Stacy saw I was a succubus, she blurted out all of her feelings for Mark and asked for my help to seduce him. It was adorable. It seems like you must have worked some magic with Mark, though. She told me he's never said anything about her appearance."

Nathan gives her a conspiratorial smile. "I may have given him a bit of encouragement."

"You two are dangerous together," I say with a soft laugh.

"Sorry for ruining game night. But it had to be done, and that lich was going to kill us all, anyway."

As excited as I was for the boss fight, I don't mind. Seeing Elle here with my friends makes me realize how perfectly she fits in my life. Now I just need to prove to her I'm an equal fit for hers.

Nathan's eyes shift toward the bedroom. "As happy as I am about our romantic victory, this is pretty awkward. Let's put some music on at least."

"Good thinking." I turn on my stereo to drown out any forthcoming sex noises and join Nathan and Elle at the table.

Nathan stops mid-conversation with Elle to take a bite of cake. "Damn, this is good!"

Elle moans as she takes a bite. "Gods, please make this for me all the time."

My cock twitches as she licks her lips, and my cheeks grow hot. "Of course. Whatever you want."

Nathan looks between us with a wolfish grin. "So, you two have any other Halloween plans? I bet you get invited to all kinds of crazy parties as a succubus."

Elle shakes her head. "I do but—"

"We're going to her cousin's Halloween party." She told me she wouldn't go this year, but I could tell she was sad to miss it.

She gives me a shocked look. "We are?"

"Yeah! I want to meet your cousin and your friends." I don't mention to Nathan that meeting them at this party will probably be while they're mid-orgy, but the thought still sends a spike of nerves through me.

"Nice, have fun!"

"You should come! Xae—my cousin—won't mind. I can ask Stacy and Mark too when they're a little less...busy." Elle grins toward the door, and I swear I can hear a breathy moan despite the loud music.

"Uh, don't you already have plans on Saturday?" I surreptitiously kick Nathan under the table and try to communicate with my eyes that he shouldn't come. I love Nathan, but I'm barely okay with going to an orgy without adding seeing my friend's knot to the mix.

Nathan doesn't miss a beat, though he gives me a pointed look that means I'll have to explain later. "Right! Yeah, I have plans. But thanks for the invite! I think Stacy and Mark are busy too..."

"No worries!" Elle says cheerily, and the conversation moves on from the party to Nathan asking Elle about her mom's home in the demon realm.

Eventually, Stacy and Mark emerge from my bedroom looking flushed and disheveled. "I'm, uh, I'm not feeling great, so Mark's going to drive me home. Great party. Nice to meet you, Elle!" Stacy doesn't give Mark a moment to say anything, tugging him after her and out the door.

"Well, guess I should head out, too. Have fun cleaning up your room!"

I flip Nathan off, but he cackles and pulls me into a tight hug.

"Elle, it truly was a pleasure to meet you. You've got a real catch on your hands, so be good to my best friend, okay?"

"He's the best. I promise I will."

I'm the best? Fuck, I need Nathan to get out of here now before I fall to my knees and beg to show her *she's* the best.

17

ELLE

As soon as Nathan is out the door, I tug Shane with me into his bedroom. I told Stacy not to use the bed, and judging by disheveled state of the dresser, that must have been where the action happened. I grin, thinking about the pair so desperate for each other finally admitting to and consummating their feelings. It's a passionate dynamic, but I'm grateful for the ease I feel with Shane.

Shane takes in the room and mutters an incantation as he goes to his bathroom, coming back with a disinfectant and rag. The room goes from smelling like sex to a pleasant fresh linen scent, and he quickly wipes down the offending wardrobe with a slight grimace. "Sorry, I wouldn't have been able to focus on anything else until I got that cleaned up."

"I'm the one who should be sorry. I got swept up in her passion and didn't think about the potential destruction to your room." I close the distance between us and wrap my arms around his neck. "How can I make it up to you?"

His breath hitches softly. "I...I want to taste you again."

Sweet, wonderful witch. Even when presented with the option of having me however he wants, he choses giving me pleasure. "Mmm, you do?"

"Y-yes. It's all I can think about lately."

"Dirty boy. Do you touch your cock when you imagine eating my pussy?" I cup his hard length through his pants and he inhales sharply.

"Gods, yes." His hips rock against my hand.

"Tell me what you think about when you come the hardest."

Shane swallows hard and flushes a bright pink. "I...uh, I..."

Interesting. There's something else he wants. "Do you remember how we talked about using a safeword?"

"Y-yes."

"First, tell me your safeword. Then tell me what you think of when you stroke that pretty cock of yours."

"*Dragon.*" The word is little more than a whisper. "I...I'm not sure..."

He's so nervous that his cock softens against my palm. I don't want to ruin the moment, but everything in me yearns to know his desires. "How about I say some things and you tell me when I get to what you want?"

"I don't think you will..."

"Use your safeword if you want me to stop. Otherwise, I'm going to ask you and I expect you to be honest with me. I want to know every dirty little thing that goes on in that mind of yours, Shane."

"O-okay."

"Good boy." I squeeze his cock and it hardens again at my words. I love how much he responds to my praise. "Let's see, you've thought about licking my pussy. What goes along with that? Oh! Do you want me to sit on your face?

Shane's eyes widen. "You're not telepathic, are you?"

"No." I laugh. "Just the next logical step in pussy eating. There's more though. I don't think you'd be so worried about asking me to sit on your face."

"I—yeah, there's more."

"Hmm, care to make a deal with me, witch?"

"Yes. Anything for you." Arousal pours off of him as I palm his cock over his pants.

"If I guess what you think about, you'll let me do it."

Shane lets out a choked sound. "I don't—you won't want to... oh gods."

I slide my hand up to tug down his zipper. "Do we have a deal? Remember, you can always use your safeword if you need to stop."

"Y-yes. Okay. You're not going to guess, but...okay."

Tugging his pants down so there's only the barrier of his boxer briefs between my hand and his cock, I resume stroking him. A wet spot from his pre-cum has already formed and I want to tug off his underwear so I can taste him.

Focus, Elle! What would he be so embarrassed about? Something that could happen while I'm sitting on his face. I can't choke him in that position. It wouldn't be conducive to any kind of impact play either, unless he's into cock and ball torture. Is that what it is?

My tail flicks behind me as I think, and Shane's eyes dart down to it, his breath quickening as he does. *My tail...what would he...*

A devilish smile forms on my face and his eyes widen. "Do you want me to fuck you, Shane?" My tail is just long enough that I could reach his ass while sitting on his face.

"Oh fuck."

"That's not an answer."

He swallows hard a few times, looking away as he gathers up courage. I wait, thoughts of filling him up with my tail while I ride his face heating my blood. It'd be even better if I tied him up, but there's no rope here.

"Fuck...yes, I—I want you to fuck me. I want you to tie me to the bed and use me. Use my mouth and fuck my ass with your tail, while I beg for you to let me come. But that's...you don't have to—"

"Take off your clothes and get on the bed." I cut him off, so turned on I can barely think.

He obeys, his hands shaking with need and anxiety as he undresses and lies on the bed. I rip off the thrown together toga and prowl over to the side of the bed, forcing myself to not just pounce on him right away.

"Elle..." He stares up at me as I approach, his pupils blown wide and his lips parted.

"There's no rope to use tonight, but you'll be a good boy and stay still, won't you?"

"Oh fuck. Y-yes. I will."

"Good. Lube?"

"Nightstand drawer. But Elle, you don't have to—"

"Are you kidding? I'm going to have so much fun filling your tight hole while I ride your face, sweet witch. Now, you won't be able to talk much while your mouth is on me, so tap my thigh twice if you need to stop."

"Okay. Gods, I can't believe this is happening."

I grin down at him. "I can. Now lie back and let me use what's mine."

18

This can't be happening. I'm going to wake up in a minute with cum-splattered sheets from the most vivid wet dream I've had in my life. But when I pinch myself, I don't wake up.

Elle giggles as she sees the movement. "It's not a dream. Though I can visit you in your sleep if you'd like."

"You can?"

"Yes, it's part of being a succubus. I avoid it because it seems wrong to take advantage of someone's sleeping mind. But I've been sorely tempted with you. Would you like that?"

Would I like to be visited by my sex goddess girlfriend while

I'm sleeping? How is that even a question? "Y-yeah. I'd like that. A lot."

She smiles as she gets on the bed next to me, running a hand down my chest to rest on my lower stomach. My cock swells, lifting and thumping down against my stomach.

"Noted." Elle uncaps the bottle of lube and pours a generous amount into her palm. "I'm going to get you warmed up with my fingers first. My tail is too thick to start with."

My entire face and chest grow hot with excitement and nerves. Oh gods, what if my ass isn't clean? I'm not one of those guys that doesn't wipe his butt, but still. "Are you sure? I-I didn't, uh, do anything to prep for this kind of thing."

"It's okay. One perk of being a succubus is that I can clean up bodily fluids and such with my magic." She rests her hand on my stomach and there's a strange tingling sensation inside of me that fades quickly. "There. Now you don't have to worry."

"That's very...convenient."

"It is! Especially for when you come inside me when we're out in public, and I don't want your cum dripping down my thighs for the rest of the date. Though that's pretty hot."

Elle winks at me as I sputter at that mental image. "If you keep saying things like that, I'm going to come before we even get started."

"No, you're not. You need to earn it first." Elle coats two of her fingers in lube and moves down my body to between my legs. She teases my cock with a soft stroke from the head to the base, then slides down the seam of my sac to rest just above my hole.

She licks her lips, violet eyes locked on mine as she circles the rim, teasing me without pressing inside.

"F-fuck, Elle..." My voice is a low whine that should embarrass me, but all I can think about is her fingers *there*. I've played with my ass a few times, but it never felt as good as this.

"If I didn't think it'd make you blow your load right away, I'd taste you here, sweet witch."

"Oh gods, you'd do that?"

"Mmm, you'd like that? My tongue playing with your tight hole, teasing you open." She presses the tip of a finger inside, drawing out a shuddering gasp from me. "That's it. Good boy, just relax and let me in."

Her finger pumps in and out of me as I clutch the sheets, trying to find something to ground me. It feels good, but what makes it overwhelming is that Elle's the one touching me like this. When she adds a second finger, my hips buck off the bed, inadvertently sliding her fingers in further and I cry out.

"Listen to you. So needy and desperate to be fucked."

"Y-yes, fuck, please." I squirm as she chuckles and removes her fingers, getting more lube and using it to slick up the spade-like tip of her tail. *Oh fuck, what is that going to feel like inside me?*

"It's going to feel good," Elle purrs as she moves up my body to straddle my stomach. I must have said that out loud, but I'm too turned on to care. "I'm going to make you feel so good, love." My heart clenches in my chest as she leans in and kisses me, her tongue inside my mouth just as urgent and desperate as I feel.

Love. She called me love.

Gods, I love her. Does she love me?

"Elle, I..." For a second, the confession sits on my tongue, but I'm too much of a coward to say it. "Please, I need you. Use me. Let me make you feel good."

Her eyelashes flutter and her pink cheeks grow rosier. Can she sense what I really wanted to say? "When you ask so sweetly, how can I say no?"

She kisses me again, then moves up to straddle my face, her perfect pussy already glistening with arousal. My hands move on their own to sink into her hips, pulling her down to my mouth. Elle cries out as my tongue touches her, bucking her hips and grinding her clit against my nose. I groan at the taste of her. Feeling her around me, covering me with her hot, wet cunt, flips a switch inside me and my hands grip her tighter, unwilling to let her take this ecstasy away from me. I devour her like a starved man, spurred on by the constant rocking of her hips and her gasps of pleasure.

Her first orgasm doesn't take long. "Oh fuck. That's so good. You're going to make me come." A gush of her arousal floods her pussy as she grinds on my face, making it hard to breathe for a moment. I'd happily die with her legs wrapped around my head, so I continue to lick her through her orgasm, both of us moaning as she comes again with a shuddering whine.

She eases her hips back to my chest and gazes down at me, flushed and wild-eyed. "Are you ready for me to fuck you, Shane?"

I stare back at her, no doubt already looking wrecked. My cock is leaking so much pre-cum that it's pooled on my stomach and I know that just a few strokes would be all I need to come. But fuck, I want this so badly. "Y-yes. Fuck me, Elle."

She gives me a sharp smile before turning to face toward my cock and easing her hips down over my face again. "Mmm, this angle will be a little tricky, but I can't resist seeing my tail sinking into you."

I moan against her pussy and she chuckles. A moment later, her slick tail is sliding against my thigh and in toward my ass. It circles my hole, stroking me over and over as Elle whispers praise. When the tip presses in, I let out a choked sound that's muffled against her and she eases her hips up enough for me to speak.

"Remember, tap me twice if you need me to stop." Her voice sounds hoarse and needy.

"Yes. I will. Please, please, I need you to—ah, oh gods!" I keen as Elle sinks her tail deeper inside me and it rubs against my prostate.

"Told you it would feel good. Now be a good boy and make me come again and maybe I'll give your cock the relief it needs."

My cock thumps against my stomach again in agreement. Elle giggles at that, then moves her tail in slow, short thrusts inside me as she places her pussy back over my mouth.

Every time the rounded edge of her tail tip drags against my prostate, I see stars. My hips strain, cock desperate for some kind of touch, but Elle grabs them and holds them down against the bed. "Definitely will need to tie you up next time, naughty boy."

My tongue flicks against her clit before sucking it between my lips and Elle makes a shocked noise, surprised when it pushes her over the edge into another orgasm. "Fuck!" Her tail pumps into me faster as she comes. She pulls off of me with a gasp and moves down my body before I can think to protest and hold her in place.

Hot, wet heat engulfs my cock as she takes it into her mouth and down to the base in one smooth movement. She pulls off, her tail still rubbing inside me. "Come for me." It only takes her two more drags of her mouth before my orgasm hits, heat roiling from deep inside me as my balls pull up and I let out a pained cry. I erupt, my cock jerking as jets of cum pulse out over and over. My whole body shakes with the overwhelming pleasure, at once wanting it to end and never wanting it to stop.

Elle pulls off me, unable to swallow down all of my cum, using her hand to pump one more stream out as her tail eases out of my ass. "That's it. Look at all that cum you gave me. Such a good boy." My cock gives a weak pulse and another spurt of cum flows out at her words. Fuck, how is that even possible that I have anything left?

Elle turns to face me and I sit up, drawing her mouth to mine, uncaring about anything but showing her how I feel right now. The taste of my release mingles with hers in our mouths, and she shivers against me. "Shane..." My name from her lips sounds like a secret confession.

"Elle...I...thank you."

She pulls back so that she can see my face. There's a hint of worry behind her eyes. "That wasn't too much? It was okay?"

"It was more than okay. You just made me come harder than I have in my entire life."

"That *was* a lot of cum." She licks her lips and grins. "Okay, you stay there. I'm going to get you some water and then we'll cuddle.

"You don't have to! I can get it." I move to slide out of the bed, but she grabs my arm.

"Nope. Part of this is you letting me take care of you when we're done. I enjoy it."

I want to protest that she should be the one being cared for and worshipped, not me. But her tone holds no room for argument. "If you want to. Okay."

She strokes a hand through my hair, sending goosebumps skittering down my spine at the tender touch. "Some day you'll learn that I never offer to do something that I don't want to do. Until then, I'm happy to keep proving it to you."

19

SHANE

The night of Xae's Halloween party arrives and I'm an anxious mess. I've spent the past two days psyching myself up for it and trying to convince myself that I'm excited to go. I want to be excited. Elle's cousin is her best friend and I need to find a way to fit in with her friends. I don't want Elle to think she has to tone herself down or refrain from doing things because I'm socially awkward and inexperienced.

Elle sees right through me when I insist I'm happy to go, but she must be able to tell that I'm determined to do this. She stopped trying to talk me out of it after our initial discussion.

How bad can it really be? We'll stop by, meet Elle's cousin and a few of her friends, and hopefully find somewhere to hang out that isn't a full-blown monster orgy. Like the kitchen. Surely where they keep the snacks is a safe-zone at an orgy.

Unlike that coven meeting, at least I know to expect group sex going into it. I heard from the paranormal council—they've sanctioned the coven and they have to have an outside observer at all of their gatherings. It's a slap on the wrist, but at least it'll keep them in line. Thankfully, I already have extreme anti-hex wards in place as a precaution for my job, in case someone from the coven wants to get revenge on me.

Dread pools in my gut. What if someone from the sex cult is at Xae's party? If I see one of them anywhere near Elle, I don't know what I'll do. I'm not a violent person and I know she's perfectly capable of taking care of herself, but the thought of someone harassing her makes my blood boil.

Thoughts spiraling, I head over to Elle's place to meet up and walk to her cousin's place. I take three deep breaths and try to shake off my nerves before knocking, and as I let out my third exhale, the door swings open.

Elle cocks a hip and gives me a teasing smile. "Do you want to come in, or are you planning on standing on my stoop all night?"

Gods, she's stunning. Tonight she has on a neon pink dress that hugs her curves in a way that makes my breath catch. It takes a while before I'm able to reply. "Just clearing my thoughts. You look amazing."

"You like the dress?" Elle does a little spin in place, allowing me to drink her in. There are cutouts in the back, placed to accommodate her wings and tail if she transforms at the party.

"Yes! It'll be a shame that people at the party won't get to see how good it looks on you for very long."

"Hah! Who said I was planning on taking my clothes off?"

Heat washes over my face. Dear gods, someday I hope I'll be

able to stop blushing so easily around her. "I, uh, I just figured since you said the party usually gets...clothing optional."

"Oh, I wasn't planning on participating in that this year." Elle sounds so casual as she motions for me to come inside that I take a minute to process what she's said.

"You won't?"

"Why? Did *you* want to? Because I'll admit, the thought of someone else touching you makes me jealous. Especially since you haven't fucked me yet."

"I don't! I just assumed you'd want to, and I'd hang out near the snacks while you have fun. Or something like that."

"You'd be okay with me having sex with other people? Is that something that turns you on? The thought of watching me with them?"

My face heats even more, but I take a moment to consider. "I'm neutral about it." Elle cocks a brow at me. "The watching part, that is! I think, uh, I think I'd at least want to know beforehand if you decide to have sex with someone else. Not to control what you're doing or because I don't trust you. Fuck, this is such a strange conversation. I guess what I'm trying to say is that I don't want you to feel limited to having one partner for the rest of your— while we're together." Shit, I almost said the rest of your life, like I'm assuming she'll want to be with me that long.

Elle surprises me when a frown twists her lips. "You're not just saying that because you're worried you won't be good enough in bed for me, are you? I know you're anxious about it, but you've made me come harder than anyone I've been with. Or is it because I'm a succubus, and that means I must not be able to control the urge to sleep around?"

The bite in her tone as she brings up being a succubus makes my stomach clench. "Elle, no. Not at all. I...shit, I didn't mean it like that. I love you as you are, and that includes you being a succubus, not in spite of it. I know you feed from work and from me, but I wouldn't want to stop you if you needed more. Or even if you just don't like the idea of being monogamous. I'm willing to share you, if that's what will make you happy."

Her mouth drops open, and she looks at me for a long moment, her eyes growing glassy. "...You love me?"

Now it's my turn to be speechless. Shit, I said that, didn't I? Too late to turn back now. "I know it's too soon..."

She takes a step closer, a tear rolling down her cheek as she smiles up at me. "You love me." It's a statement this time.

"Yes. Gods, I love you, Elle. You're the most wonderful person I've ever met. I know it must sound crazy, but I love you. And I know that love can only grow the more time we're together. I understand if you don't feel—"

"I love you, Shane." Another tear slides down her face, and she laughs as I cup her cheek to wipe it away. "I've wanted to tell you, but I was worried you'd think I was nuts. Turns out we both are."

My breath whooshes out of my lungs at her words, and my eyes fill with happy tears. *She loves me.* "Yeah, I guess so."

Elle licks her lips, her expression growing serious again. "Thank you. No one has ever been so open and accepting of my succubus nature."

"You don't have to thank me, Elle. You're perfect, exactly as you are."

Her eyes fill again. "So are you. I don't want to sleep with anyone else. I know it surprises people, but I'm monogamous. A wild orgy every so often when I'm single? Sure. But when I have a partner, that's who I want. I want you, Shane. Only you."

"Oh." I open and close my mouth a few times, trying to formulate a response other than that, but nothing comes out. So I pull her closer and let my body tell her how I feel instead.

The moment our lips touch, she lets out a shuddering exhale and wraps her arms around me. The kiss is tender and filled with everything we've left unspoken until now. Our love. Our dreams of a future together. Elle deepens the kiss, her hand threading through my hair like she's afraid I'll pull away. But I'm not going anywhere. I'll stay for as long as she wants me.

When our lips part, Elle lets out a soft chuckle. "Wow. So *that's* what being loved feels like."

"Y-yeah. I'll be happy to keep showing you later, but we should probably head out if you want to get to Xae's party before everyone's already naked."

"Fuck Xae's party. I want you to show me *now*. I need you, Shane. *All* of you." She punctuates her words by grabbing my ass and pressing my cock into her belly. "Are you ready for that?" she asks, her voice softer.

I groan as she drags her lips against my neck, but for the first time, I'm not nervous. I want this. I want to give her everything she needs. "Fuck yes."

"Thank the gods." Elle turns around and places her hands on the island counter, pressing her hips back to show off her lack of panties. "We'll have time for lovemaking in bed later. Get your cock out and fuck me. *Now*."

I scramble to obey, unzipping my pants and tugging out my dick as fast as I can. It's already rock hard as I position myself behind her, running a hand up her thighs and pressing it between her legs. "You're so wet."

"I'm ready for you. Fuck me, Shane. Don't make me ask again."

My hand shakes as I draw it back and slick my cock with her wetness before lining it up with her entrance. I say a silent prayer to whatever gods will listen, asking them to help me not to come the second I'm inside her, then thrust inside in one deep stroke.

Elle moans and the air punches out of my lungs at the incredible sensation of being sheathed inside her. "Oh f-fuck. Elle, you're so...fuck!"

"Breathe, love. You're not going to come until I tell you to."

I listen to her, taking a few deep breaths until the urgent need to come passes. I can do this for her. "I'll be good for you."

"I know you will. Now move."

She gasps as I obey, pulling back and thrusting in again. She grins over her shoulder at me, lifting a hand from the counter to tug the neckline of her dress down and free her breasts. When I thrust again, they sway from the movement and suddenly all I want is to see how hard I can make her tits bounce as I slam into her.

I grip her hips and pump into her in deep strokes. She feels like heaven around my cock. Too damn good, but I can hold out longer for her.

"Harder!" she moans, pushing her hips back to meet each thrust. "Oh fuck, you feel so good, Shane. I knew your thick cock would fill me up so well."

"*Shit.* You feel incredible. I don't know how much longer I can... you're too good."

One of Elle's hands drops from the counter to work her clit. "Just a bit longer..."

I grit my teeth, knowing I'm on the precipice of my orgasm, as I continue to slam into her. "Right there, oh gods, yes! Come for me." Her channel clenches around me as she comes and as soon as the words escape her lips, my release begins as her pussy milks my cock.

I cry out as my cock jerks inside her with the first jet of my release. Elle moans, feeling my orgasm along with me. "Mmm, yes, that's it. Fill me up with your cum. I want you to breed me."

"Oh fuck." Her filthy words are too much and I gasp as I do just as she asks.

When my hips finally still, I let out a shell-shocked laugh. "Holy shit, Elle."

"You've got that right," she says with a weak laugh that tells me she's just as affected.

She shivers as my cock slides out of her, glistening with an obscene mixture of her wetness and my cum. My cock gives a feeble twitch as I watch some of my release slide down her thighs.

"Like the look of your cum dripping out of my pussy?"

"Y-yes."

"Mmm, dirty boy. I bet you want to fill me up again, don't you? Breed my pussy over and over."

Oh gods, there are those filthy words again. "Breed?"

"Yes, Shane. I didn't know that was a kink of mine until now, but fuck, it makes me hot thinking of you breeding me. I don't want you to knock me up for real. Don't worry. At least not yet." She winks at me, laughing at my shocked expression.

Against all odds, my cock stiffens again at the thought. "I...I can do that."

"I know you can. Now, go upstairs, get undressed, and wait for me on the bed. I need to call Xae to let them know something's come up."

20

ELLE

"Hey, where the hell are you? I want to meet your man before things get too crazy!" Xae's voice shouts over the thudding music and conversation in the background.

I hold the phone back from my ear, wincing. "We're not coming, I'm sorry."

"What?"

I repeat myself, louder this time, and Xae gasps. "Why not? Oh shit, did something happen? If Shane did anything to hurt you, I'm going to murder him—party be damned."

"He told me he loved me."

"What?!"

A huge grin forms on my face. "He told me he loved me."

"Wow, Elle! *Wow*! You love him, right?"

"Of course I fucking love him! You know I'm obsessed with him." I'm shouting just as loud as Xae now.

They laugh. "Just checking. Have fun with your *love*. Try not to kill him with too many orgasms in one night."

I think about Shane currently waiting for me up on my bed. "No promises there. Have fun with the orgy!"

Hanging up the phone, I take a moment to bask in tonight's events. Shane loves me. He loves me and he finally fucked me. All I can think of is how many ways I can show him I love him back. And how I can drive him wild tonight.

I grab two glasses of water and a bag of trail mix before heading upstairs. The door to my bedroom is open and the sight of Shane's pale skin gleaming in the dim light as he sits completely naked on the bed makes me desperate for him again.

"Are we taking a snack break?" Shane's lip twitches as he looks at what's in my hands.

"We're going to be in here for a while, so I figured I'd be proactive."

"Beautiful *and* smart. I'm the luckiest man in the universe."

I set the snacks down and unzip my dress, letting it pool on the floor, then kick off my heels. "Damn right you are."

Shane swallows heavily as he takes in my naked body with the same awe as the first time he saw it. I lick my lips and smile back at him, then touch my spellmark to shift into my succubus form. Sex feels great when I'm in my more human form, but it's incredible when I'm fully myself. I just hope the differences don't surprise Shane too much.

"Figured I should give you the full succubus experience now that you're no longer a virgin."

"I thought you said that virginity was a construct!"

I laugh as Shane frowns at me. "I did, but I also like the idea of corrupting a sweet, innocent witch into giving me his virtue."

Shane huffs out a laugh, but his cheeks grow pink. "I...I want you to corrupt me."

My pussy clenches as I move to the bed. "I know you do, dirty boy."

His lips part, already flushed and breathless from our conversation. "H-how do you want me?"

I let my eyes rake over his lean torso and down to his cock, which lies swollen against his stomach, still glistening from earlier.

"On your back. I want to ride you."

"Fuck, yes." He scrambles to lie back, and I have to resist the urge to giggle at his eagerness.

I straddle him, enjoying the devotion and desire in his eyes as he gazes up at me. I know that same look is reflected in mine. "Mmm, you look so good like this. I can't wait to feel you inside me again."

"Gods, I can't believe you're mine." Shane gasps as I grasp his cock and slide it between my folds, teasing the tip against my clit before lining it up with my entrance.

"All yours. Just like you're mine. Before we do this, I need to ask you something."

He blinks up at me, his cock throbbing in my hand. "Anything."

"What do you know about sex with a succubus?"

Shane's brow furrows. "Other than what we've done together, not much. I know you feed from my desire and when I come, you can feel it. Is there more?"

I hesitate for a second, then shake away my worries. Shane won't freak out. He loves me. "When I'm in this form, there's, uh, stuff inside me."

"Oh." Shane tenses up and I sense a slight dip in his arousal. "Like teeth? I don't know if I'm into pain, but I'm happy to try it out. As long as you think it's safe."

I snort. "You really *do* love me. No, not teeth. You don't need to worry about shredding your dick."

"Whew, okay." Shane chuckles, sliding his hands up to hold my hips. "I can't think of anything else that would be inside you that might be an issue. Whatever it is, you can tell me. Or make it a surprise. Just...can we please keep going?"

"Hah! You fuck me once and now you're impatient to get back inside me. Alright, surprise it is!" With no more warning, I sink down on him to the hilt, and we both gasp at the sensation.

Shane's eyes open from when he reflexively shut them, no doubt subconsciously still worried about vagina dentata. "I don't —you don't feel any different."

The slit inside me just above my g-spot opens and my tendrils press against it, eager to wrap around the cock inside me. Easing my hips back up, I give them room to extrude and Shane gasps in shock as they spiral around his cock.

"F-fuck, you have *tentacles*?"

They tug on him in response, pulling him back inside me as I lower myself onto him again. Each time they rub against him, a pulse of pleasure surges through me. "They're to keep you from escaping me until I'm done with you, sweet witch."

"Oh gods, fuck that's—it feels...Elle!" Shane's broken words spur me on and I moan as I ride him in earnest. The obscene slick sound of my tendrils and pussy sliding against his cock and our cries of need building my arousal higher and higher. It's been so long since I've done this. I forgot how *amazing* it is.

"You like being trapped inside of me? Mine to fuck over and over until I'm satisfied."

"Y-yes! Use me, *please.*"

It doesn't take long for me to reach my peak, screaming out as it crashes over me. Unlike in my other form, it just keeps going and going as my tendrils squeeze around Shane's cock and my pussy pulses, needing to feel him come too.

"Fuck! I'm going to come."

"Give it to me." I gasp, the pleasure heightening even more as his cock surges inside me and fills me with his hot cum. I writhe on top of him, mindlessly riding out our shared pleasure.

When I come back to my senses, Shane is gasping my name and shaking beneath me as my tendrils give him one last squeeze before retreating. I ease off of him, even though I'm so high on him I could ride him all night long and never tire. He looks utterly wrecked, so we'll have to work up to that.

"I...I..." Shane opens and closes his mouth a few times, before shaking his head.

"Too much for you?" I ask the question with a light smile, but there's a pang of worry in my gut.

"Never." He pushes himself up to sitting and wraps has arms around me, holding me in his lap. Any worries I had dissipate as he holds me with such tenderness. When we part, he gives me a soft smile. "Though I think I might need that snack break before we go again."

AFTER WATER AND SNACKS, we go again. And then again. One of the best parts of being a succubus is that my magic reduces the refractory period Shane would normally require, so he can fuck me as many times in a row as I need.

Once the frenzied desire burns off, our joining turns languid, Shane rocking inside me as we hold each other. When I'm sated, I shift to my human form, and he wraps himself around me, whispering worshipful words as he strokes my hip and stomach. Showing me love and adoration I've never experienced before.

Tears prick at my eyes for the second time tonight. This is what it feels like to be loved. To feel like I'm cherished and enough for my partner. To trust someone and know that I'm safe in their arms.

"I'm so glad that sex cult summoned me," I whisper.

Shane huffs out a laugh against my hair. "Me too."

His breath slows behind me, no doubt on the verge of falling asleep.

"Shane?"

"Mmm?"

"When we get married, I want four kids. And at least one pet."

His hand stroking my stomach falters for a second before resuming its motion. "Sounds perfect."

"Shane?"

"Yeah?" He sounds a little breathless now.

"You've got the nicest dick I've ever seen."

He laughs, the warm sound sinking into my chest. I want to hear that sound every day for the rest of my life. "Wow, thank you. You're not just saying that because I agreed to four kids, are you?"

"No, but it's a nice perk if I'm sticking with you. Thought I'd let you know."

"*If* you're sticking with me?" He squeezes me closer, arms tightening like he's afraid I'll pull away.

"Sorry," I giggle. "I can't make that call without you at least meeting my cousin. They're the last word on if you deserve me."

"Shit. Are they free tomorrow?"

I turn in his arms and press a kiss against his chest. "I'll call them in the morning."

21

SHANE

"I-I've never done this in front of anyone before."

Elle's lips brush against my ear as she leans in to whisper, sending a shiver down my spine. "Don't be shy, love. You can do this."

"Is there anything I can do to help? Do you need me to hold your wand or something?" Nathan shouts from the kitchen as he finishes washing up the dishes from our dinner together.

"Yeah, do you need him to hold your *wand*?" Xae flashes a grin identical to Elle's. Their presence fills up my small apartment despite their petite frame. When they arrived earlier, they immediately tugged me into a crushing hug and proclaimed that I was "the cutest little nerd they'd ever seen."

I roll my eyes at Nathan. "I don't use a wand for my magic."

"I don't know, your wand makes me feel pretty magical." Elle grins sweetly at me as color floods my face.

"Oh gods, you two are just the cutest couple ever!" Xae proclaims.

Nathan nods. "I know. It's kind of sickening."

I clear my throat. "I should probably get started with the ritual."

"I'm so excited! Thank you for letting us be a part of this, Shane." Elle kisses my cheek and some of my nerves dissipate.

When we woke up after our night of intense, life-altering sex, Elle called Xae to see if they were free for dinner. She insisted I invite Nathan, saying it was only fair for us both to have someone important to us there to give their approval. At that moment, I realized Nathan *is* the most important person in my life besides Elle. My parents live across the country and don't agree with a lot of my "lifestyle choices" and I have no siblings or other family to speak of. I almost cried when Nathan arrived and gave me a big hug. If he noticed, he didn't say anything, which I appreciated.

It was only when I was halfway through prepping dinner that Elle realized it was Samhain. I tried to tell her I could skip my spell-work for the year, but once she brought it up, everyone was so excited about the idea of helping me with a ritual that I couldn't argue.

So here I am, lighting candles and prepping the material components while they eagerly await a demonstration of my magic. Too bad it won't look like much.

They gather around the small illusory magic circle I made on my living room carpet, eyes gleaming with interest in the low light.

"Alright." I take a deep breath and focus on Elle's warm thigh pressed against mine. "We're here tonight, joined by friendship and love."

"Aww, dude! You love me?" Nathan interrupts, and Xae smacks his shoulder, shushing him.

"Uh, so tonight the veil between this world and the world of spirits is thin. That makes it the perfect time to reach out to our ancestors for guidance and to recognize and embrace the smaller deaths that happen in our mortal lives."

I glance around at everyone, and Elle nods encouragingly. "I, um, I don't have any skill in communing with the dead, though. Sorry! I thought I could create some enchanted tokens that will help to support and protect us through those smaller deaths to help us through changes as they come."

"Whoa, you can do that?" Nathan's impressed reaction makes me think the idea isn't completely lame. "Magic is so cool! Damn, I'm jealous. All I get is strength and too much body hair."

"That sounds lovely, Shane," Xae adds, their full lips twisting into a smirk. "It makes me wish I didn't immediately think of la petite mort when you said small deaths."

I flush, but Nathan claps me on the back. "Man, if those tokens can make our orgasms better, that's even more rad!"

"It's not—that's not...I'd need to study more sex magic for that, sorry."

Elle winks at me. "Maybe next year. You do have that book."

The chances of me ever casting from a spellbook that made me have a perma-boner with no release are slim, but I shrug. "Uh, maybe."

Elle's sweet laugh washes over me and I have to resist the urge to lean into her.

"Alright, here goes nothing. All I need you to do is think about the changes and transitions in your life and close your eyes." The eye-closing isn't necessary, but since the spell doesn't have any visually interesting components, I'd rather not have them staring at me the whole time I'm saying the incantations.

They all obey, closing their eyes. After a couple of seconds, the energy in the room changes from teasing to something more charged. As I say the first line of the spell, lighting the taper in front of me, my magic tingles up from my core, down my arms, and into my hands. The smell of petrichor and electricity fills the room as I move to the next line of the incantation. With the next line, potential buzzes through me, my magic ready to infuse the rings with protective energy. And with the final words, I direct the energy to flow out of me.

The candle flickers, and a phantom breeze spirals through the room, rustling through Elle's hair. Goosebumps prickle against my skin with an awareness that something or someone is here with us, aiding in the casting. Whether it's a spirit or just the collection of paranormals here within my magic circle, I don't know. But as my magic wanes, I truly have the sense of being guided from one phase to the next by a gentle, loving force.

I let myself sit in that sensation for a minute before snuffing the candle. "Okay, that should be it."

"Wow, that was fast!" Nathan grins at me as I pass his ring over. "Nice. Maybe it'll help me find a girlfriend."

I resist the urge to tell him it doesn't work that way. "Uh, maybe!"

Xae rubs their slender arms like they're trying to get rid of a chill. "Did you feel that energy at the end? That was so cool, Shane."

"I'm glad you liked it! Hopefully, this will be at least somewhat helpful for you." I hand them their ring.

I turn to Elle to find that she has an awed expression on her face. "Can you two give us a minute?"

"Oh! Sure." Nathan scrambles to his feet and offers a hand to Xae.

"You said something about dating troubles?" they ask Nathan as the pair heads off to the kitchen, giving us some privacy.

I place a hand on Elle's arm. "Are you okay?"

"I'm wonderful." She leans in and kisses me, her tongue swiping against mine before pulling back. "Just wanted a moment alone to do that."

"I don't mind if you kiss me in front of other people." My mind is already fogging with desire after that quick kiss.

Elle gives me a wicked grin. "Noted."

I hand Elle the remaining ring. "I, uh, I added something to yours that I've been meaning to do for a while."

"Oh?" Her lip twists. "Did you save the orgasm magic just for mine? Because I think I'm good in that department."

I snort. "Nope. It's a ward. Now that I'm Xae-approved and we're having four babies..." Elle laughs, her sparkling eyes dazzling me for a moment. "Uh, I wanted to protect you in case some assholes try to summon you again. So I warded you against summoning. I can do the same for Xae if they want, but I didn't want assume anything."

Elle's eyes widen. "That's...out of all the sweet things you done, this is possibly the sweetest. Thank you, Shane."

She pulls me in and presses a soft kiss to my lips. "Thank you for rescuing me the first night we met."

She kisses me again. "Thank you for calling out the coven to the paranormal council."

Another kiss, deeper this time. "Thank you for protecting me."

One last lingering kiss that makes me ache for her. Her voice wobbles. "Thank you for loving me."

"Elle...You don't need to thank me. You deserve everything. I'm just the lucky bastard that gets to try his best to give it to you."

I tilt my head down to kiss her again, but Nathan's voice cuts through the moment. "You two lovebirds going to stop making out at some point? It's time for pie!"

Elle laughs and wipes away the moisture from her eyes. "Coming!"

As we sit around the table, Elle's hand clasped in mine as we eat pumpkin pie and Nathan and Xae try to one up each other with double entendres, that sense of passing from one phase to another washes over me again.

I squeeze Elle's hand tighter. I can't wait for what this next phase holds if I get to share it with her.

EPILOGUE

Forty years later

"So there I was, standing with my tits out in front of a group of sex cultists, and then I heard this voice. Strong and indignant, with a hint of nerves. And somehow, in that moment, I just knew—"

Max, my youngest, turns bright red, and he hides his face in his palms. He looks so much like his father did at that age when he's embarrassed. "Mom, I love you, but you don't have to give us a blow by blow of how you and Dad met and fell in love every Halloween."

"Yeah, especially not the blow by blow part," adds Samantha with a snort. My youngest daughter loves a good innuendo.

Nathan laughs and waves dismissively at her. "That's the best part!"

"You *would* like that, pervert." She scowls back at him and flips her platinum hair over her shoulder. It looks like she styled it special for tonight. For a moment, I have the urge to pry into her emotions to find out why, but I learned years ago to keep that boundary up with my kids. As much as I love to tease them, they don't need their mom knowing all their strong emotions.

Shane frowns. "Don't be rude to Nathan. He traveled across the country just to celebrate the holiday with us."

"Probably because he doesn't get enough action, so he needs to hear your gross sex stories again to jerk off to later."

"Samantha!" Shane gives Nathan an apologetic look and I have to bite my tongue to keep from laughing at the quip.

The handsome werewolf laughs and waves him off. "It's fine! Sam's right, I don't get a lot of action these days."

There's sadness behind his eyes despite his joke, something that's steadily built since we first met. I can sense how much he craves connection. Over the years, Shane and I have talked offhand about asking his best friend to come live with us if he's still a bachelor by the time all our kids moved out. That time has come and gone, so maybe we should have a serious discussion about it. We're both worried about him living alone. He needs people that care for him in his life. Not just an asshole business partner and a bunch of fancy cars.

"I don't think you're pathetic, Uncle Nathan." My darling Claire pats his arm and gives him a gentle smile. No doubt she senses the pain behind his words even more than I can, being the most powerful empath in our family.

"Thanks, sweetheart." He smiles back at her, then winks. "You're my favorite, you know."

She quirks an eyebrow at that, reading something I can't pick up on.

"Claire, you're 35. You don't have to call him uncle any more. He's not related to us!" Samantha huffs, rolling her eyes at her sister.

Maggie, my eldest, elbows her in the ribs. "Leave her alone. It's sweet. We love our wonderful, though distant, *Uncle* Nathan. Right, Max?"

"Of course. As long as he keeps Mom from continuing her love story, Uncle Nathan's the best."

I clap my hands together and grin back at the rest of the table. "Speaking of which, where was I?"

Max groans and gives me a pleading look. "Other families have cute holiday traditions. Pumpkin carving or apple picking. Why does ours have to involve you reminding us how much you guys banged back in the day?"

"Your father and I *still* have a very active sex life. It's a beautiful and vital part of a healthy relationship as a succubus." I hide my grin as all four of my children groan in unison.

Shane squeezes my hand under the table and chuckles, and I feel a hint of desire thrum through me. Gods, even after all these years, I've never stopped craving him. Time slows as he gives me a loving smile that crinkles the corners of his eyes, and for a moment, it feels like that very first night we met.

"What's that about your sex life?" Xae's voice calls out, cutting through the moment. A second later, they appear in the dining room, looking stunning as always.

"Xae!" My girls all squeal in excitement that they've arrived, and Max gives a wave and a soft smile. While my girls think it's gross to talk to me about sex, they confess everything to Xae. I'd be jealous, but it makes me so happy that they have a connection with them and a source of knowledge about their succubus nature. I just wish my sweet Max would take advantage of Xae's guidance, but he tries to ignore his succubus side, so I don't press him on it.

"My favorite little demons!" Xae kisses each one of my kids on the cheek, smacking Nathan's head playfully when he leans in like he's asking for a kiss, too.

"Damn, did I miss hearing the story of how you fell in love? Sorry I'm so late. I got a bit tied up." Knowing them, they mean that literally.

"Your timing is perfect. Elle was just getting started." Shane stands to pull out their chair, ever the gentleman, even after all these years.

"I think I'll go get started on the dishes," says Max, pushing up out of his chair. His sisters all proclaim that they want to help. The only time they all work together is to get away from me embarrassing them. It's been a handy tool in our parenting arsenal.

Nathan holds a hand out to Max. "Before you run off, I meant to ask—how's Devon doing? He hasn't called me in a while. You two have been practically attached at the hip for years, so I figured you could give me an update on my elusive nephew."

Max stiffens, and his face falls for a second before masking into a pleasant smile. "We, uh, we haven't spoken much since I decided to relocate to Moonvale. But I'm sure he's doing fine. If I hear from him, I'll tell him to call you."

"Oh, that's right! When's the big move?"

"Next week."

Shane and I exchange a quick glance. Neither of us wants Max to leave, but he's an adult. If he thinks it will help him get some distance from the city and his family, that's okay. As the baby of the family, I know he's always felt like he's in the shadow of his sisters. But I'm going to be so sad not seeing him every few days when he's at the PI office or over for family dinner.

Once again, Samhain reminds me that change and the death of what once was is an inevitable part of life, like Shane said so eloquently during our first one together. Our children are grown and living their own lives. Max leaving feels like the final step of that transition.

The kids scurry away to the kitchen and Xae and Nathan start to chat, giving me a moment to focus on my husband.

He leans in to kiss my cheek. "You have a serious look on your face. What are you thinking about, my love?"

"Our family. Change. What comes next."

"It all feels like it's happening so fast, doesn't it? One minute you're confessing love to a woman you met a couple of weeks ago, and the next your children have grown up and are moving away."

I sigh and lean into his shoulder. "Hmm, guess now that the kids don't need us, I could go out and find an upgrade. The same cock for forty years is a long time..."

Shane laughs and kisses my hair. "Whatever makes you happy. Though, I will miss you. We could spend a thousand lifetimes together and I'd never tire of you. But you're a goddess and I'm just the lowly witch that you let worship you."

"Mmm, maybe I'll allow you to earn your place at my side for a bit longer. If you worship me to my satisfaction tonight."

His breath hitches, and I taste his desire. "Thank you for your generosity, my love."

I laugh and kiss him, resisting the urge to linger against his lips while guests are sitting across the table. "I love you, sweet witch. I would gladly spend a thousand lifetimes with you, too."

Want more more monster romance? Sign up for my newsletter to get bonus content and the latest news on upcoming releases.

Read on for a sneak preview of Behold Her, my spicy paranormal romance featuring a plus-size FMC and a monster MMC that blends dark themes with humor and heart to create a spellbinding story of transformation and love.

BEHOLD HER

I've always watched people. According to my mother, it started the moment I was born. A normal crying baby for but a moment before my wide, dark eyes took in my surroundings in silence. She swears I was born to see things that others can't, but that's just the wishful thinking of a doting mother who wants something extraordinary for her child. If I truly had the gift of sight, I wouldn't be where I am now. I would've seen the betrayal and heartache that blindsided me.

Pulling into a parking spot on the sunny, tree-lined street outside a quaint apartment building, I let out a sigh. The nice weather is a stark contrast to my mood these days. I can barely make it through a day without my mind wandering to *them*. And that leads down the rabbit hole of self-loathing. I know what happened wasn't my fault. That doesn't stop my mind from torturing me with impossible what-ifs. What if I hadn't jumped into things so fast? What if I'd had more control? What if I was someone else?

A yappy bark snaps me back to my surroundings. *Enough.* I'm here to work, not wallow in my dark thoughts. An elderly couple walking a pair of pomeranians passes by my car, followed by a teenager on a bike. No one spares a sideways glance to acknowledge my presence.

Good. That means this is a neighborhood where everyone's too busy worrying about their own little worlds to pay attention to who comes and goes. It'll make my job easier.

I pull on a baseball cap to cover my unkempt hair and grab a to-go bag from a local Chinese restaurant that I picked up on the way here. Hopping out of my nondescript silver sedan, I stride up and down the sidewalk, scanning apartment numbers. 611, 612... here we go, 613.

I circle the building, pretending that I haven't found my target yet. Getting a layout is important for any gig, even if it's only surveillance. No external staircases and no alternate exits for each unit, other than a small porch or balcony. I'll have eyes on whoever comes and goes from 613 even from my parking spot on the street.

Well, this certainly won't be my most challenging job. It's ridiculous how little people around here seem to notice or care about their privacy. Blinds open, with no regard who can see inside. They must feel secure in the mundanity of their lives and the "safe" neighborhood they live in.

Safety and privacy are an illusion. After years of working as a private investigator, I've faced that sobering truth time and time again. Sometimes I wish I lived a normal life, just so I could walk through life with oblivious naivety. But I've seen what lurks in the darkness. Hell, I *am* what lurks in the darkness to many people.

I'm not just talking about my job—which admittedly involves a lot of creeping around in the dark and monitoring people. I'm a monster. In the most literal sense—I'm half-succubus and half-witch. Succubus, not incubus, since most monsters did away with unnecessary gendered names centuries ago.

Humans don't know that monsters exist. And while most paranormal beings just want to live in peaceful hiding, that doesn't change the fact that we're the creatures that fuel their nightmares.

With that cheery thought, I force my attention back to apartment 613. The blinds are open to the kitchen and living area, but the lights are off. There's enough late-afternoon light streaming in that the occupant could be home, but after a few minutes of observation, I'm certain they're out. Looks like I'll be spending a while longer in this slice of domestic mundanity.

If I'm lucky, I'll get all the evidence I need tonight and won't need to come back. Snap a few pictures of a cheating wife with her lover and satisfy my client's need for irrefutable evidence of infidelity.

As I'm settling in for hours of waiting, my cell buzzes in my pocket. I fish it out, a pang of dread mixed with foolish hope in my stomach. I release my tense breath when I see Claire's name on the screen, and answer. "What's up? I'm working."

A brief snort rings in my ear. "Hello to you too, Max!"

I roll my eyes, thankful she can't see me. "Hi Claire. What's up?" I ask again.

"Can't a girl check on her baby brother? I haven't heard a peep from you since you left the nest. Is Moonvale everything you dreamed it would be?"

My teeth grit at her teasing tone, but I know better than to let her lure me into her trap. I've had 32 years to learn that lesson. If I show any sign of frustration, she'll pounce. "It's fine. I'll call you tomorrow and tell you all about it if you're really interested and not just digging for gossip. But like I said, I'm working."

"Hah! We both know that if you're working and still answering your phone, that means you're stuck in your car with nothing important to do. Completely at my mercy." I can sense her glee through the phone.

Claire loves to keep tabs on me, always trying to find juicy tidbits about my personal life to present to our sisters and parents. She takes the role of family gossip seriously and takes particular delight in revealing my secrets. Though I'm pretty damn good at choosing what I let her see and keeping important things hidden. That's how no one knows the real reason I moved away from home.

With no excuse on hand to get out of the call, I give in and endure her loving, ruthless interrogation into my personal life. I tell her about my bland, cookie-cutter rental house. I assure her I've made at least one friend—the beagle I pet when out on my morning run counts as a friend, right? Work is fine. I'm fine.

That last one is a lie. As a skilled empath, she must sense hurt simmering under the surface of my words even through the phone. She asks again for the real reason I left the city, her cheerful voice dipping into concern. The unstated question of why I'd leave our family, a well-established client base, and close friendships behind hangs heavy between us. The truth is too embarrassing and painful, so I provide her with the reason I've crafted—with the rapid growth of Moonvale's paranormal community, it's the perfect place to expand Pearce Investigations. Everyone else in the family has strong ties to home, so I was the logical choice to take on the endeavor. She sounds like she wants to argue, so I redirect her with a question about her daughters' exploits before she can.

Though I pretend to only begrudgingly endure the conversation, we both know that I appreciate the chat. That I need the connection, even if I say I'm okay being on my own. I've been in Moonvale for a little less than a month and now that the novelty has worn off, loneliness is setting in.

Sometimes—usually late at night when I lose the battle to keep my sadness at bay—I think moving was a mistake. In the process of cutting myself off from heartache, I cut out all the bright spots in my life. But running back home after barely a month away isn't an option. I have to move on. At least in this boring town where no one knows me or what kind of monster I am, I can be anyone. I can finally be free of all the implications and expectations that go along with being part-succubus.

The sun dips below the horizon by the time my call with Claire ends. Not long after, a white SUV pulls into the designated spot for apartment 613. I shift down in my seat, pretending to be on the phone again while I watch a man emerge from the car. He slams the door shut behind him and stomps his way to his door. Once inside, he flips on the lights, giving me a good view of him through the windows.

Average height, thin, salt and pepper hair that's balding in the front, sallow skin, and tired eyes. Perfectly average. Not who you'd imagine a beautiful faun would choose to ruin a fifteen year marriage on an affair with, but looks aren't everything. I'd have to interact with him directly to sense if he's paranormal himself, but that could explain his appeal. The romantic in me hopes that the faun's wife was wrong about the affair, and this guy is just her accountant. The realist knows all signs point to the faun cheating with him.

I watch him as he rips off his tie and grabs a beer from the fridge, letting the bottle cap fall on the floor when he pops it off. He heads into the living room and turns on his television, downing half the beer with a grimace. It doesn't take long before he's finished that beer and on to the next. Then a third. When he screams obscenities at his tv, so loud that I can hear them through my open car window, I'm positive tonight isn't a date night.

My eyes dart up to the apartment above his, wondering how his upstairs neighbor feels about the disruptive behavior. Their blinds are angled, but the bright lights against the darkness allow me to see inside fairly well. This apartment is a stark contrast to the sad bachelor pad below, filled with cheery color and life.

I've always enjoyed seeing how people choose to decorate their home. It can tell you a lot about them. Though in my case, my rental home screams serial killer with the blank walls and bland furnishings, and I'd like to think I'm neither bland nor creepy. What I can see in apartment 623 fills me with a sense of whimsy and something about it calls to me deep in my gut in a way I don't understand. At least not until I see who lives there.

Time stops.

My breath catches in my throat as a woman emerges from a side room. Inky black hair piled atop her head, she cinches the belt of a thin robe that doesn't cover much of her golden brown skin and ample figure. She looks down at her phone as she wanders into her living room absentmindedly. For a moment, she turns toward the windows, allowing me to drink in the low neckline of her poorly tied robe. A small smile twists her lips at whatever's on her phone.

Nothing about this woman should be notable to me. I've seen countless attractive people in my line of work in far more compromising situations, and felt nothing. But my whole body tenses as I watch her, as though she holds the secrets to the universe inside her. My mind, body, and soul yearn to uncover the truths hidden within her. And just like that, in an instant, my fiendish nature that I've tried so hard to escape rears its ugly head. The spark of desire takes root before I can stop it.

Shit, this is going to be a problem.

Want to read the rest of the story? Behold Her is available now!

- Monster MMC (part witch/part succubus)
- Plus-Size FMC (human)
- Dark(ish) Stalker(ish) Romance
- Spicy Magic Dreams
- BDSM
- Misunderstandings/Bad Timing
- Hidden Identity
- Healing Past Trauma

AUTHOR NOTE

Hello! Thanks so much for reading Maneater. I hope you enjoyed this introduction to my new monster romance series, Monsters of Moonvale. If you didn't, that's okay! We all love different things and I still appreciate you taking the time to read my book.

I hadn't planned to write Maneater. But when I was working on edits of Behold Her (my upcoming dark-ish monster romance), I kept thinking about how fun it would be to tell the story of how Max's parents met. Finding your partner at a sex cult demon summoning is a unique meet cute that begged for more exploration. As soon as I started writing about Elle and Shane, I fell in love with them. There's just something so delicious to me about a shy cinnamon roll guy and a woman who takes control.

You'll see a bit more of Shane and Elle in Behold Her, but that book focuses on their son Max and a new character, Mona. Behold Her is a much darker and more emotional story than Maneater, but they both share the same humor, heat, and heart.

Huge thanks to my beta readers, Amber, Angelina, Courtney, Holly, Lauren, and Lindsey. I couldn't have written Maneater without your feedback and insights. And of course, thank you to all my amazing ARC readers! I'd be lost without your support and encouragement.

Thanks again for reading and for your support!

ABOUT THE AUTHOR

Emily loves cozy, emotional, and spicy romances with a monstrous twist. When she isn't musing on the merits of doting, dominant monsters, she works on her spicy D&D podcast, reads an obscene amount of romance novels, and cultivates her eccentric recluse persona.

www.emilyantoinette.com

Made in the USA
Middletown, DE
26 August 2024

59272160R00102